MIXED OUT

THE MIXED GIRL SERIES BOOK TWO

LAMONIQUE MAC

MIXED OUT

For information email: lamoniquemac@themixedgirlseries.com

Cover Design by: Terry Cooper

ISBN: 978-1-7354287-3-4 (paperback)

MIXED OUT

For all the princesses that don't know they are one.

ALSO BY LAMONIQUE MAC

The Mixed Girl Series

Poor Little Mixed Girl (Book One)
Mixed Out (Book Two)
Snakes in the Mix (Book Three)

SIGN UP FOR MY NEWSLETTER

Be the first to learn about LaMonique Mac's new releases and receive exclusive content for fiction readers.

www.authorlamoniquemac.com

CONTENTS

BROTHERLY ADVICE

Bishop and LaMonica were rolling down the back streets of the East Side hood in Saginaw. Bishop had ditched his Chevette for a blue Chevy Nova. LaMonica was still passionate about the conversation they had had at home. Bishop's cousin Lucas was cheating on his wife Renee, and apparently, not only was she still letting him use her for money, but he had put his hands on her and beat her up as well. None of this stopped her from wanting to be with him, however.

Lucas and Renee were the talk of everyone in their circle. Becky (Alonzo's wife) and LaMonica had already discussed it, and even B had discussed it at home with LaMonica.

"Man, I don't know what cuz is doin'. Renee is a good woman. Every man will test what's out there, though. See, that's why you're lucky. I don't even go out there and cheat on you when you're on your period or nothin', like most men would," Bishop told LaMonica.

These statements Bishop made were working on LaMonica's frustration level. B was constantly trying to remind her of how lucky she was to have a "good man" by lowering the bar further and further to the ground. After all of Mama's teachings, LaMonica felt very strong and passionate against letting a man use her or put his hands on her. And having one that didn't wasn't a privilege; it was the bare minimum.

When they were leaving the house and walking to the car, LaMonica was intensely trying to get her points across to Bishop.

"I mean, Bishop, how could Renee allow a man to do this to her? How can she be so stupid? I bet you it couldn't be me."

Whenever LaMonica got passionate about something, she tended to go on and on about it. And so, like a dog with a bone, she chewed on and on about Lucas and Renee's relationship like it personally affected her. As they rode along in the car down East Genesee Street headed to Bishop's aunt's house, she continued going on and on, making her point about how stupid this girl was being and that she would never, ever be that stupid.

"LaMonica, that's them people's business. If she wants to stay with that man, you ain't got nothin' to do with it, so just drop it."

"Well, I bet you I wouldn't let no man run me around like that. If a man EVER put his hands on me, I would leave him in a heartbeat."

The next thing LaMonica knew, she felt a hot slap across her face. She grabbed her left cheek with both hands, looking at Bishop with pure shock. Time seemed to stop. She could hear her every breath.

Everyone had said Bishop would turn out to be like this, especially Ms. Demona. It was the last words she had uttered to LaMonica as she was packing up and moving out of Mama's upstairs apartment to marry her longtime boyfriend.

"I can't wait to hear about when that nigga starts beatin' yo' ass, LaMonica." Demona moved out of town with her new husband, and LaMonica never had to be bothered with her again.

Never had Bishop put his hands on her before that day. Time seemed to stand still as she sat there stunned, continuously holding her cheek, looking at him with eyes wide open like, *what the heck, man?*

They pulled into Bishop's Aunt Frieda's driveway on South Park Street, where she lived as a resident in the group home her granddaughter owned. Bishop parked the car.

"Look here; you ain't going nowhere. I just had to let you know with action. So now you know. My brother taught me that when a woman gets to talking about 'how she's gonna leave if somebody hits her,' you go ahead and hit her across the face. That'll be the final answer to her 'I'm gonna leave threat.' If she ain't going nowhere, she can shut up and never say that again. Now I dun taught you a lesson today. And you ain't going nowhere, so you can shut up about it and don't let that come out yo' mouth again. Now I bet you won't say that no mo'."

LaMonica exited the car with Bishop to go inside Aunt Frieda's house to pick up their baby girl, Monica. They always stayed and visited with Bishop's aunt because she was enjoyable to be around. Usually, LaMonica and Aunt Frieda would get into lively discussions about something on TV or play a round of cards. But this time, LaMonica was exceptionally quiet during the visit. She just quietly smiled at Aunt Frieda and left with Bishop and the baby.

She had indeed learned a lesson that day. Bishop had done the unthinkable. It didn't surprise LaMonica that

Alonzo would give Bishop this kind of advice because he was quite the womanizer and user of women. He would often come by the house, remarking on how he's able to use his wife for all her money while banging some of her friends at the same time. He bragged about these things right in front of LaMonica.

"Yo' B, check this out. Becky's about to get her income tax money back, and they called me instead of her to pick it up. Yeah, peep that. That's about to be all my money now."

Another time Alonzo came by bragging about his drinking tales.

"Yo' dig this B, last night me, Becky and her friend Harper all got drunk together. Becky passed out, and Harper tells me, 'if you got a condom, I'll bang you while she's sleep'. You know I had to do it, right?"

LaMonica was right there while Alonzo was telling these stories. He acted as if they were all in on something together against his wife, Becky. LaMonica could never imagine Bishop acting like his brother. Even though Bishop was hood, he had heart. They seemed to be polar opposites in personality—until now.

Whenever Bishop's brother came over with his stories, LaMonica hated him with every word he spoke out of his mouth. Alonzo might've been pretty in the eyes of a lot of women, even in his downgraded state from his fine days when he was younger, but he was ugly on the inside. He had the heart of a person with the evil ways. He had even tried to attach himself to LaMonica's friend Kristina when his wife went out of town for work. LaMonica hated the fact that she was associated with Alonzo because it caused her friends to be associated with him too. Kristina had been through enough already, and sometimes it was hard for women to see past Alonzo's light skin and wavy hair. She hoped Kristina didn't get caught up in his web.

No, Alonzo certainly hadn't changed much since getting out of prison. In fact, he was a scary dude. Back when LaMonica was pregnant, he had been shot while engaging in an argument on the street. The guy he was arguing with had a rifle, and instead of running or trying to get away like most folks would, Alonzo kept advancing towards the dude, trying to take his gun. The guy shot him, leaving a large hole in his arm.

Alonzo had an evil sort of bravado. This made LaMonica hate him all the more and distrust him. She hated having him around. But she couldn't do much about it. The house they lived in belonged to both him and Bishop. Their Aunt Frieda had bought it for them when they were kids living on the streets. Alonzo lived with his wife Becky, but he could come back there any time he wanted to. Besides, Bishop looked up to Alonzo. He had practically raised him from the time he was 13 years old. He could do no wrong in his eyes. The only thing about Alonzo that Bishop hadn't emulated up until this point was how he treated women.

That's why Bishop taking his brother's advice on smacking women into place, after all they had been through, surprised LaMonica so much. Bishop was more of a lovable person. He was so charming LaMonica had chosen Bishop and their baby over everything and everyone else. Over the advice of her mother, her friends, over the directions of her own doctors. She had even lost Daddy because she refused to have the abortion.

This had all been Bishop's idea. Create a baby together to get out of Mama's house. Move in with him and get on welfare. Against all odds, she had followed his plan. And now this! Maybe Luchie had been right. LaMonica should've never moved out of her mother's house just to get on welfare with a man. No matter how much Bishop said he loved her, some of his actions just didn't lineup with what was right.

Let's see how we got here.

2

SISTERLY LOVE

W hen LaMonica had gotten past the point of being able to end her pregnancy and kept the baby, Mama seemed to begin to accept it. Her biggest concern was for LaMonica's health and well-being. But she was unrelenting in unforgiving Bishop for impregnating her daughter.

"I don't want that nigga nowhere around here, LaMonica, and I mean that," Mama would say.

LaMonica honored Mama's wishes and didn't have Bishop over to the house. But every day, while she was at work, LaMonica would make her rounds walking. First, she would walk over to Bishop's house around the corner; then, she would go and spend time with Luchie and Amalia at their home.

On days when Bishop had told her he would be at his mom's house for the day, LaMonica would stay home so she could talk to him on the phone while Mama was at work.

One afternoon while Mama was working, and she was waiting for a call from Bishop, LaMonica received a phone call from the State of Michigan Department of Social Services.

"Hello, is Mrs. Power's there?"

"No, she's not home. Can I take a message?" LaMonica asked.

"Yes, please tell her that the Department of Social Services called, and we've found the person she requested."

"Wait, is it my sister Ambrosia Copeland?"

"Is this LaMonica?"

"Yes."

"Yes, honey, we've found your sister. She's living with members of the Copeland family in Detroit. Have Mrs. Powers call me today, and I'll get all the information over to her."

"Okay, I will."

Mama often called in during her lunch hour to check in with LaMonica, or sometimes she would even stop by the house for lunch. She'd often become angry when she would come home, and LaMonica wasn't there. She knew most likely she was around that corner with Bishop.

Well, this time, Bishop was at his mom's house, so LaMonica wasn't going anywhere. Besides, she couldn't wait for Mama to come home so she could tell her that the woman from the Department of Social Services called and they could get in contact with her sister Ambrosia.

Mama came home for lunch that day. While she was making a quick sandwich, LaMonica told her the good news.

"Mama, the woman from Social Services called. She said they found Ambrosia. Mama, can you call her back now, please?"

"I can't call her back now, LaMonica, or I'll be late for my patient. I'm gonna grab this sandwich and run. If I have time between patients or get off early enough today, I'll swing by there and see what they have. They usually have a report set up. I'll talk to my friend Kim from Parents Without Partners (PWP) who works there."

LaMonica could hardly wait for Mama to get off work. She hoped it would be early enough for her to go down to Social Services and get her sister's info.

Mama made it back in the door at 4 p.m. She had gotten off work early enough, and she had the information on Ambrosia.

"Here's the paperwork. They have a phone number too. Kim checked it for me, and it's working. If you want to call her, we can. I'll call and talk to the adult she's living with."

"Okay, Mama."

Mrs. Powers called the 313-area code number in Detroit. A woman answered, and Mrs. Powers explained she was LaMonica's adoptive mother, and she was looking for LaMonica's sister, Ambrosia. The woman on the other end said she was Ambrosia's sister-in-law, Vanda. The man who had raised Ambrosia as his daughter Clovis Copeland had moved to California to run a massage parlor, among other things. Ambrosia had been back and forth between Clovis' family members ever since.

Ambrosia knew about LaMonica already. She had been told about her from their mother, Angie, years ago when she was little. The man who raised her also told her about LaMonica in mocking ways whenever she was in trouble as a child. She hoped they would meet, but did not know if that would ever happen. This phone call was a complete shock to her.

"Hello." Ambrosia got on the phone and was a bit timid.

"Hi, Ambrosia."

"Is this LaMonica?"

"Yes, this is your sister."

The girls awkwardly met each other over the telephone. LaMonica and Ambrosia were both teenagers. They weren't even a full year apart. They were eleven months apart, to be exact. As soon as Mama went into the next room and Vanda also left Ambrosia to talk on the phone privately, the girls began to hit it off.

It was easy for them to talk about all sorts of teenage things. Detroit was fashion forward and Ambrosia knew a great deal about all the trends. This was on her mind a lot. LaMonica had begun to come out of that phase as she was more focused on becoming a mother.

Ambrosia couldn't really call long distance on someone else's phone, but Mama made sure the girls could talk to each other several times a week. They grew closer and closer.

When LaMonica told Bishop that she had found her sister, he was so happy for her.

"I can't wait to meet her baby," Bishop said.

"Well, I may go down to Detroit to visit with her B."

"Yeah, baby, you should go visit yo' sister if you can. That's family. You need to meet yo' family."

It surprised LaMonica at how understanding Bishop was being, since he usually was jealous about those sorts of things.

"I'll let you know before I go down there."

"Bet that," Bishop said.

Soon after their conversations began, Ambrosia upped and moved into Clovis' brother's house, her Uncle Miles. Miles lived in a Detroit two-story flat with his girlfriend. The more Ambrosia and LaMonica talked on the phone; the more LaMonica wanted to go to Detroit and meet her sister in person. Mama began speaking with Miles on the phone to get a feel for the situation if she allowed LaMonica to visit Detroit. After speaking with Miles, Mama decided to let LaMonica go and stay with her sister for the weekend.

Ambrosia's move to Miles' house worked out for their mother, Angie. After losing Ambrosia to Clovis and his family, Angie was out of the loop about her whereabouts for years. She was often walking around the city of Detroit from one end to another, and as luck would have it, she upped and discovered Miles' home one day while walking. When Ambrosia moved into Miles' flat, Angie came by one day only to find her daughter was there, and they were reunited.

Angie began visiting with Ambrosia frequently throughout the week now that she was living at Miles' house. LaMonica had even spoken to her on the phone during one of her conversations with Ambrosia. Angie was very excited that LaMonica would come to visit Ambrosia soon, and she would have both of her daughters in one room.

The most pressing question LaMonica had for Angie was, "*Where is Jackie? When can we see Jackie?*"

"LaMonica, he's in an orphanage. They let me visit him once a week."

"Well, I want us to visit him when I get there," LaMonica said.

Angie seemed to dodge LaMonica's conversation about visiting her little brother. LaMonica decided she would bring it up again once she was in Detroit. If her little brother was in an orphanage, she wanted him out. She was getting ready to move out of Mama's house and go live with Bishop when she turned 17. Maybe they would let her get him. LaMonica decided that the next time she visited with Bishop, she would ask him about it.

On LaMonica's next visit to Bishop's, she asked him about her brother.

"Bishop, my brother is in an orphanage in Detroit. When I move in here, I want to get him and adopt him."

"Oh no, not me, LaMonica. I'm not takin' care of nobody else's kid but my own."

Bishop seemed very serious. She could see it was something she couldn't bring up again. She was being denied at every turn. First from Mama and now Bishop. LaMonica felt so limited. *How am I ever going to get my brother?*

The weekend finally came for LaMonica to visit Ambrosia in Detroit. LaMonica was about five months pregnant at this point and clearly showing. When they pulled up to the two-family flat in Detroit, LaMonica and Ambrosia met and hugged. Mama stayed for a little while and met Miles and his live-in girlfriend, Pearl.

LaMonica had everything she needed for the weekend. When Mama was getting ready to leave for Saginaw, she looked at LaMonica, "Are you sure you're okay with staying here?"

"Yes, Mama, I'll be fine," LaMonica said.

Right away, LaMonica noticed that Ambrosia and the tenants in Miles' house went to the store a lot. It was just down the street, and all day Ambrosia would ask Miles for money to run down to the store to grab a bag of chips, a soda pop, candy, or whatever.

Everything in Miles' house was nice too. He had lovely furnishings that were newer and lots of gold-colored décor. It reminded LaMonica of Daddy's home. Miles had a nicer, newer refrigerator too. It had double doors and an ice maker on it. It was shiny and pretty, but not much food was stocked in it. Ambrosia said they liked to buy their food the same way by running down to the store each time they ate.

LaMonica found that to be extremely odd and told Ambrosia as much. Ambrosia argued that this was the best way.

"Okay," was all LaMonica could settle on for agreement. But being pregnant, this flustered her.

Ambrosia and Miles had lots of friends and family from the neighborhood who liked to stop by. Imagine LaMonica's elation when one of those visitors at the door finally turned out to be her mother, Angie.

LaMonica was very excited to see her mother. They had talked on the phone, but it had been years since they'd seen each other in person. Ambrosia was a little less than enthused. She had been seeing Angie frequently and had come to find her a source of irritation, especially since she had dropped a bombshell right before LaMonica came to Detroit.

"Ambrosia, now that your sister is coming down from Saginaw, I just want to let you know that you and her have the same father."

"What do you mean we have the same father?" Ambrosia asked.

"Chuck Price is not only LaMonica's father, but he's your father too," Angie explained.

In all of her 15 years, Ambrosia had never heard this. She mainly had been living with either Clovis or his family her whole life. As a matter of fact, she was closer to them than she was to Angie. When Ambrosia lived with Clovis, Angie would have to sneak up to her school to even try to see her. She once tried to take her back again from Clovis but that didn't work out.

When Clovis met Angie, she was pregnant and showing. When he was done with Angie, he let his new girlfriend play the motherly role in Ambrosia's life. Clovis didn't even allow Angie to see her own daughter most of the time. Ambrosia didn't understand that Clovis had outright taken her from her mother. But LaMonica did.

Mama and Daddy had both explained it to her a long time ago. Daddy had received horrible reports of the things that happened to Ambrosia due to her living with Clovis. The only reason Mama had let LaMonica stay with his brother Miles was because he seemed to be stable, and Clovis was nowhere near around.

Ambrosia idolized Clovis, even though his chosen profession was pimpin' women. He had taught her everything she knew from her foundation. He taught her to, "Always be number one. Get that money above all else. You've got to get yo' hands on what you want in life. And don't ever be the one to 'get got.' Above all else, make sure you look good doing it, girl!" Clovis would say.

Fancy clothing and shiny cars were very important to him, probably even above basic necessities. That was to his and anybody else's detriment around him who didn't comply. He had a stable of ladies in his heyday that made sure he was living "right" and fat off the hog.

Mama had told LaMonica of the night Clovis had shown up at her door in the middle of the night at the big yellow house on 5th Street. She said LaMonica was just a little girl, and Clovis was trying to convince her to release LaMonica to him. Mama said he was dressed like a pimp in a fur coat with a cane and a pimp hat. It was undeniable what Angie was doing for him.

"I'm with Angie now, Mrs. Powers, and we're here to get LaMonica so we can raise both our girls together."

He obviously didn't know Mama. She wasn't the type to be pressured by anybody. She told him he could get up off her door, but if they wanted to leave Ambrosia, they were more than welcomed to.

Angie left Chuck back in the '70s when she was big and pregnant with Ambrosia. He had taken to putting his hands on her, and he was often messing with other women and young girls, including Birdie. Angie had had it for the last time and decided to leave permanently. For some reason, she chose Detroit as a getaway spot. She was young, gullible, and had an undiagnosed mental health disorder. Angie was just ripe for the picking for someone who believed in "gettin' 'em before you get got."

Angie had been **got**. She became one of Clovis' sex workers and eventually lost her child to him. The more LaMonica tried to explain this to Ambrosia, the less she wanted to hear it. She even tried to offer her proof by telling her all the stories that Aunt Bren, Daddy, and Mama had said about him (that he wasn't her father—that he took her from Angie—that Chuck Price is her real father). All of this effort was lost on Ambrosia.

When Angie was there visiting with them, she came and sat at the table with the two girls. She told Ambrosia the truth AGAIN! Ambrosia refused to believe it AGAIN. LaMonica just couldn't understand how Ambrosia couldn't see what she had known most of her life, that she was conceived in Saginaw. Mama had physically seen Angie leave Saginaw for Detroit BIG and PREGNANT. She passed that info on to Ambrosia. Aunt Bren and Daddy had stories of Angie taking off all the time when she was already pregnant and then finally staying gone in Detroit. She also gave that information on to Ambrosia as proof.

What man would try to claim a child that wasn't his? Daddy had more than enough kids to claim. He didn't need to make up an extra one. Here their mother Angie was telling Ambrosia herself, "Yes, Chuck is your actual father," and Ambrosia just shut it all out.

Being a teenager and also never walking in Ambrosia's shoes before, LaMonica felt angry that Ambrosia wanted to hold on to this lie so firmly. Whenever anyone would come by the house and remark on how much Ambrosia and LaMonica looked alike, LaMonica would quickly explain, "that's because I'm her sister. We have the same Mama AND THE SAME DADDY!" Ambrosia didn't like it and told her as much.

LaMonica let it go, and when she did, she and Ambrosia enjoyed each other's company again. LaMonica was happy to be around her real mother and her sister. She resigned (for the moment) that sometimes you just can't make people look at the truth.

Restoration of families can be complicated. It can have highs and lows that an adopted child didn't anticipate. LaMonica was learning that this weekend.

3

UNMIXED

Angie came over daily while LaMonica was in Detroit. She observed Angie's mind state. Her biological mother had the mental capacity of a child. She often told them inappropriate sexual stories about her and her boyfriend. She laughed and giggled like a child when following them to the store for Ambrosia's daily store buys. She would recite Ambrosia's entire first and middle name whenever addressing her.

"Ambrosia Jennay, Ambrosia Jennay. I want something from the store. Can you buy me something from the store?"

Angie would begin picking up random food items from the store and asking Ambrosia to buy them for her.

"Ambrosia Jennay, can I have this?"

"No, put that down!" Ambrosia would yell at Angie and respond as if she were talking to a child.

"What about this Ambrosia Jennay? Ambrosia Jennay, can I have this?" Angie would grab another object. Her voice would become increasingly nasally each time she did this.

"No. I'm not buyin' that," Ambrosia would respond.

The whole scene was like watching an out-of-control toddler with a parent in the store. The girls began running from Angie so she wouldn't do this. She would run behind them down the street chanting, "LaMonica and Ambrosia Jennay."

It became their running joke with each other to repeat Ambrosia's name in a nasally voice and say, "Ambrosia Jennay."

It was a little embarrassing for both Ambrosia and LaMonica to deal with Angie at the store and out on the street. LaMonica remembered Daddy saying that she had turned "crazy" because somebody had put something in her drink. LaMonica was pretty sure it was much more than that.

Angie kept her meds with her when she walked all around the city of Detroit because she never knew where she might end up spending the night if she stayed out too late. She took strong meds like Haldol and Lithium. Angie said she was diagnosed as Manic Depressive/Bipolar. She often went off her meds, though. LaMonica felt this was probably the general reason she wasn't able to care for her children.

"Why don't you stay on your meds?" LaMonica asked Angie while they were seated at the table.

"They make me feel funny, LaMonica."

"Yeah, but maybe if you stayed on your meds, you could get Jackie back."

"Have you ever taken mental health medicine, LaMonica?"

"No," LaMonica answered.

"I have to struggle to do anything on psych meds. Sometimes I have to fight to even be able to talk."

LaMonica thought about it. She would not like that.

"Well, when can we go see Jackie?"

"Jackie is on the other side of Detroit."

"So, I wanna see my little brother."

"Here's a picture of him."

Angie pulled out a picture of Jackie in a baby swing at the orphanage. She was standing by him. Ambrosia and LaMonica both grabbed at the photograph. They both wanted to see their little brother.

"Let's get on the bus and go see him now!" LaMonica passionately requested.

"LaMonica, I told you the orphanage is all the way on the West Side."

LaMonica was getting upset at this point. It sounded to her like Angie was just making excuses.

"You walk all over this big city any other time. Every day. Why can't we go see my little brother? If we leave now, we can catch the bus."

"LaMonica, I can only see your brother on certain days, and besides, he's getting ready to be adopted."

So, it was too late then. Too late for her to get her little brother. He was going to be adopted.

LaMonica decided to ask Angie more family questions while she had her at that table. She'd never had an opportunity like this before.

"What about the rest of our family on your side? Where are they?"

"My mother's in Battle Creek, Michigan. I took you to meet her when you were a baby, and she said she didn't want no half-Black baby sleeping in any of her beds."

"So, what did you do?"

"I had to put you in a drawer for the night so you wouldn't be on her bed."

LaMonica's eyes bucked, and her mouth dropped.

"You mean you stayed the night, and you made me sleep in a drawer?"

"Well, what else was I supposed to do, LaMonica?"

"You leave! You take your baby, and you leave! You don't make your baby sleep in a drawer and spend the night at a house with people who don't like her because she's half Black. You leave!"

LaMonica couldn't believe it. With each passing hour she spent with Angie, she realized she would have been incapable of raising her. She just wasn't mentally fit. LaMonica kept repeating to herself; *it's not her fault. It's not her fault. She's mental; she's mental. It's not her fault.*

There was a deep anger in LaMonica after hearing how her grandmother and White family felt about her. Ambrosia was just looking on quietly during this entire time, like it didn't personally bother her. LaMonica had been the child who knew Daddy. LaMonica had been the child who had met Angie's mother. None of this seemed to affect Ambrosia whatsoever.

Ambrosia had always been a part of Clovis' family. Even though she was at least two shades lighter than LaMonica and had the nickname in the Detroit hoods of "White girl," she embraced more of what is popularly thought of as "the Black culture." Ambrosia grew up in Detroit the hood way - point, blank, period. She hadn't had the exposure to White culture LaMonica had from suburban schools and Mama's friends and extra-curricular activities.

After hearing how Angie's family felt about her, that they hated her because she was half Black, LaMonica decided she would hate them too. She didn't want to be half White anymore. She was gonna get all the mix out. If anyone asked her, she was gonna be Black, just like Ambrosia.

Not only was she gonna be Black, but she was gonna be fist raising, Black power proclaiming, hair braid wearing Black. She was gonna be **BLACKITY BLACK.**

4

A GOOD BABY-DADDY-TO-BE

LaMonica returned to life in Saginaw. Despite the highs and lows of meeting her sister Ambrosia and getting to know her biological mother, Angie, she left Detroit with the overall feeling of happiness to have connected with them both. She now had a sister. She couldn't wait to share the news with B.

LaMonica was getting closer to 6 months of pregnancy when Bishop got one of his old cars running and started picking her up so she wouldn't have to walk around to his house. The neighbors reported it back to Mama, and once again, she reiterated, "LaMonica, I've done told you I don't want Bishop at my house."

The bigger LaMonica got with her pregnancy, the more she needed new clothes. She began to ask Mama for them. On those days Mama's switch would flip. She would become angry that LaMonica was pregnant all over again.

"Mama, I need some maternity pants."

"Well, have that nigga to get you some maternity pants," Mama would say.

LaMonica would go to B, and he would always have an

excuse as to why he didn't have any money to help get anything for her. Or anything she asked him to buy in preparations for the baby, for that matter. Bishop was full of a lot of love for LaMonica and the baby, but not much action.

"Love don't pay no bills," Mama would often say.

Mama was almost the opposite of Bishop. She would appear harsh and make statements like, "tell that nigga to get it," but she would usually end up going to pick up the items that LaMonica needed. Mama just wanted to show her she was the one that was truly there for her, not Bishop. He was just like she had said before, "an ain't bleep ass nigga."

LaMonica decided she wouldn't push Bishop so hard about the things that *she* needed. But she did expect him to at least contribute towards the baby's needs. Time would tell how that would work out.

Bishop continued to pick LaMonica up in front of Mrs. Powers' house daily while she was at work. The neighbors would always report this back to her.

"LaMonica, you gonna get that nigga hurt if he keeps coming around my house."

At first, LaMonica and Bishop didn't pay Mama's threats any attention. During the Summer, whenever she was working with a client, they would sneak around together and ride to parks and through the hood like they always did. But Mama had the neighbors watching the house. They would report back to her that LaMonica had left with Bishop. Mama went so far as to get a restraining order on Bishop because LaMonica was still a minor at 16.

In September, when school started back up, LaMonica attended Ruben Daniels Lifelong Learning Center, an alternative school for pregnant teens, high school dropouts, and adults who needed a diploma. Ruben Daniels differed from OIC (LaMonica's last alternative school) because it had classes that catered to pregnant and new moms. They offered Labor and Delivery Childbirth Classes and Child Education Classes. They also had a daycare center so teens could bring their babies with them and continue school after giving birth.

Bishop signed up to attend Ruben Daniels right along with LaMonica. Once Mama had the restraining order, it was the easiest way for them to see each other. Plus, the State of Michigan had given out an order that anyone receiving General Assistance (GA)—(welfare for adults without children) had to attend some sort of classes to continue receiving their benefits.

LaMonica loved taking Childbirth classes and Child Development classes with B. Bishop was one of the few fathers who attended these classes with their pregnant girl-friends. As a matter of fact, he was one of the few young black fathers in Saginaw that LaMonica knew of who hadn't left their pregnant girlfriend.

At first, Mama had no idea that Bishop was attending the same school as LaMonica. But somehow, her super sleuth kicked in, and she figured it out.

She showed up during lunch hour one day, waiving the restraining order. Mama walked right up to LaMonica and Bishop while they were having lunch.

"What the hell are you doing here around my daughter, Bishop? I have a restraining order, and your ass is going to jail."

Mrs. Powers started cussing Bishop out. It was embarrassing. Bishop just stood there. He didn't argue with her. When she got forceful with him and demanded a response, he would just say, "okay, Mrs. Powers, okay."

The entire incident was so loud, the school police came over to see what was going on.

"What seems to be the problem, ma'am?" one officer asked.

These weren't the same police officers that Mama knew. They didn't work the beat on the streets like her police friends. They had strictly only worked in the Saginaw Public School buildings; therefore, she didn't have the same kind of pull with them. In truth, the Ruben Daniels' police officers were pretty cool. They were all young and were even friends with some of the adult students. One officer often gave B dap (fist bumps).

"Look here, I have a restraining order, and I want you to do something about this." Mrs. Powers was clamoring for the officers' attention.

"Ma'am, Bishop is a student at this school; we can't remove him. He's just sitting here eating lunch, and he hasn't done anything wrong."

"Look right here. This restraining order says Bishop Holmes has to be at least 300 feet away from LaMonica Powers at all times. Do you see that right there?"

Exasperated at their complacency, Mama asked with authority, "You know what, as a matter of fact, where is yo' boss?"

"Alright, hold on, Mrs. Powers. I'm sure we can take care of this.

'Bishop, you can start eating lunch on the second round in order not to be in the lunchroom when LaMonica is here. Go ahead, go back to class. You can come back on second lunch."

Bishop stood up from the lunch table. He and the school officer looked at each other like they had a secret agreement.

They were doing this all for show to get Mrs. Powers off their backs.

As Bishop was leaving, Mrs. Powers continued cussing him out.

"That's right, get on out of here. B%@# What are you doing having your ass in this lunchroom anyway, aren't you supposed to be on the adult side of the school?"

"Okay, Mrs. Powers, okay. You're right," is all Bishop would say as he was leaving.

Mrs. Powers left satisfied.

LaMonica felt controlled by Mama. She wanted to be with Bishop even more after that incident. He had handled it so well, not even cussing Mama back out or anything. She didn't think she could've been so nice if it were his family.

What LaMonica didn't understand was that Bishop was methodical. He constantly analyzed the odds against him before acting. He knew he didn't want to cause a commotion with Mrs. Powers or the school campus police. She had a legally binding, restraining order. And even though he was only 2 ½ years older than LaMonica, he was still an adult, and she was a minor. The school police were cool; as long as he kept things calm, he and LaMonica would be back to their regularly scheduled program the next day. He would let Mrs. Powers have her shots, but once LaMonica was living with him, it would be his turn.

LaMonica was an idealist, and her emotions led to her decisions. Everything Bishop did seemed to be phenomenal to LaMonica when compared to most of the dudes in the hood. He was right by her side for the pregnancy. He even tried to attend her ultrasound appointment, but Mama had come storming up in there waiving around her restraining order and had him kicked out of there too. Bishop Holmes was a good baby-daddy-to-be. They were battling for something together. They were fighting for love. What a pull! Nothing was stronger than that.

LaMonica was completely wooed, which would ultimately guide her decision to continue in the plan to leave Mama's house with Bishop.

Bishop loved LaMonica as well, maybe even deeply, but he would never let it override the overall goal. And the overall goal was always to calculate how to get more money.

After the school incident with Mrs. Powers, Bishop and LaMonica continued seeing each other at school, but they missed doing fun things outside of that. It became challenging for Bishop and LaMonica to see each other outside of class because of Mama's grip.

One Saturday, when Mrs. Powers had some extra client work, she and Bishop snuck off in his new car to the park. He had a cousin who was willing to let him take over the payments from a mid-'80s model Buick. It was the first time Bishop had ever owned a car that wasn't from the '70s.

Bishop called from his mother's house to let LaMonica know he was on his way.

"Get ready, baby. I've got the whole day planned out for us. We're going to go out to the park and grill since it's still nice outside, then bend a few corners in the new ride."

LaMonica was ready as soon as he pulled up. She jumped in, kissed B, and was ready to go.

"Wow, baby, look at you, you're getting bigger and bigger. My baby is growing up strong inside of you." B rubbed LaMonica's stomach and kissed the baby inside.

Then they just sat there, with Bishop looking at her.

"Hurry, B; we've got to go before some of Mama's neighbors see us."

"It's the weekend baby, who are they gonna call?"

"Yeah, you're right, Mama's office is closed, and they

don't have the direct number for her client. But still, I would feel better if we hurried up. Why are you staring at me?"

"Because you've got to take better care of yourself and our baby, LaMonica. We're not pulling off until you have your seatbelt on. Here let me put it on for you."

Bishop reached over LaMonica and secured her seatbelt.

"I've got to take extra care of you now baby, you've got my child inside of you."

LaMonica blushed. *Wow, B is so caring.*

They rode to the South Side of town to Wickes Park near the Parkside Projects. Becky and Alonzo joined them. Alonzo could be almost human acting during these barbeques. They played music, ate good food, and joked around. It was easy to forget (for a time) what a monster Alonzo really was.

Bishop, Becky, and Alonzo were all drinking 40 oz beers. LaMonica sipped on juice. She didn't even drink soda while pregnant or eat candy bars because she wanted the baby to be as healthy as possible. The doctors already suspected that the baby inside of her would have the same heart defect as LaMonica. They wouldn't be sure until the baby was born, though, so LaMonica wanted to give her baby every possible advantage for a good outcome.

Alonzo and Becky packed up to pick their son up from the sitter, leaving Bishop and LaMonica some space to be alone. As evening drew near, Bishop and LaMonica decided to use their alone time in the park for what it was known for—sex.

It had gotten much later at that point, nearly 7 p.m. Mama was sure to be home and off work. LaMonica knew she was already in trouble, so she said forget it and stayed even later at the park with Bishop. Bishop and LaMonica were holding each other while listening to the music play in the car when Mama rolled up on them.

"Dang, how the heck did she know I was here?"

"Get yo' ass in this car, LaMonica."

LaMonica didn't budge, so Mama came and started grabbing on the passenger side door handle.

"I said open this door, LaMonica."

"Calm down, Mrs. Powers. Don't be comin' at her like that."

"Look, you mind yo' own business, Bishop. This is my daughter, and you ain't got no business having her out here at the park, anyway."

Bishop followed Mrs. Powers and LaMonica home. He wanted to make sure she was safe. An overwhelming protective instinct had risen up in him since LaMonica's pregnancy. Whenever they could get away to walk anywhere, he always made sure she was inside of the street, away from cars. He was protecting her, and he was protecting his baby.

5

THE WRONG BASEBALL TEAM

B ishop could see that LaMonica and Mrs. Powers
were arguing on the way home. Inside of the car,
hormones and emotions had taken over LaMonica.
Everything had become too much. She had no control over
her own life. She began reliving all the things Mama had
done throughout her pregnancy that made her feel helpless
and controlled by another human being—starting with the
ultrasound incident. That one had hurt the most.

LaMonica had to have several ultrasound appointments
because the doctors and specialists were checking to see if
the baby she carried had the same heart defect that she had.
Mama had accompanied her to all of them and had ultrasound pictures and everything. For the final ultrasound,
LaMonica wanted to include Bishop. He was so in love with
the baby already. She wanted him to have that experience.

On the day of the ultrasound, LaMonica told Mama she
already had a ride to her appointment. Surprisingly, Mama
didn't argue and just said, "okay."

Bishop's car was down, so Aunt Frieda had come during
school and picked LaMonica and Bishop up for the ultra-

sound appointment. Bishop and LaMonica were all cozy in the ultrasound room. The tech revealed they were having a girl. Bishop was overcome with emotion.

The tech began typing "hello Daddy" in cute tiny bubbles above the baby's pictures. She told Bishop she would later print them out for him. LaMonica and Bishop were so happy when suddenly, they heard a ruckus out in the hallway. Mama came bursting into the room, waving her restraining order paper in the air. There were about four staff members from the doctor's office with her, trying to quiet her from disturbing the other patients. Someone must have let it slip which room LaMonica was in.

"I want him out of here now!"

"Mrs. Powers LaMonica has rights. If she wants the father of the baby to be here, she can choose to have him at her ultrasound appointment," a staff member explained.

"What rights? LaMonica is a minor. Besides that, I have this restraining order, and he isn't supposed to be within 300 feet of her. I want him out of here now."

The office staff didn't seem to agree with Mama, but she was disturbing the patients, and technically she had that restraining order, so they asked Bishop to leave.

Mama came and selfishly stood in Bishop's place. The ultrasound tech slowly deleted all the references to "Daddy" in the bubbles above the baby and replaced them with "Hi Grandma."

LaMonica just turned her head towards the wall and mentally exited the whole ultrasound experience. *Why did Mama agree to let me get my own ride in the first place? B's car was down, but obviously, she surely must have known someone in B's family was probably bringing me. It's as if she wanted some big ta-da, gotcha moment.*

LaMonica felt an extreme level of frustration at not

having control over who could see what was going on in her own body. Mama was so selfish she had seen multiple of these ultrasounds. Why couldn't Bishop see just one?

The more LaMonica thought about that ultrasound appointment, the angrier she got.

Then there had been the baby shower. Mama was gracious to throw it, but she wouldn't allow any of B's family to come. It just made no sense. *Why was she doing this to separate her from the father of her own child? The incident at the school was totally embarrassing, and now this.* LaMonica began speaking to Mama in a disrespectful tone.

"How did you know where I was, anyway?"

"I went looking for you when you weren't at home. I checked every park until I found you. And when you get home, you'll have some explainin' to do to the police, because I called you in as a runaway."

"What?" LaMonica said with shock.

"Yep, sure did. You'd better hope they don't take you back to Juvenile. That's what you get for acting grown."

LaMonica had gone to Juvenile when she was close to 4 months pregnant. She had gotten angry at Mama and threw a bottle of hair oil at her. Never did LaMonica actually expect for it to land, but it did. The hair oil bottle hit Mama right in the forehead, and she had a bump.

Mama called the police out. But she really was just using them as a scare tactic. She didn't really think they would lock LaMonica up. The police showed up and informed LaMonica they would be considering the hair oil bottle as a weapon, and she was being charged and sent to Juvenile.

"Can't I go to Innerlink, the runaway shelter?" LaMonica asked.

"No, honey, you've committed a crime now. You're going to Juvenile," the female police officer said. Even though she was taking LaMonica to lock up, she was still nice. At least she didn't make her wear handcuffs.

As they were riding, they made their way near downtown to the Police Precinct.

This isn't Juvenile; why are we here? LaMonica thought.

"Okay, come on. Get on out. We're going in," the officer stated.

LaMonica made her way inside the Police Station she had been to many times before with Mama for her Police Community Relations Commission meetings. They headed upstairs, and she was placed inside an interrogation room.

"Wait here. Someone else is going to drive you to Juvenile," she said.

In walked LaMonica's cousin, Uncle Charlie's son, Charlie Jr.

Obviously, Mama had called up to the station and told him what was going on. Charlie Jr came into the interrogation room to let LaMonica know what her options were.

"So, you hittin' your own Mama with bottles now, huh?" Charlie Jr asked.

"And you're doing all this just so you can go out with that lame?"

LaMonica rolled her eyes at him.

"Hey! You know yo' Mama gave me permission to beat yo' ass, right?"

When that didn't work, he tried a softer tactic.

"Look, I'm sure Aunt Ella Mae will drop all these charges if you just sign some paperwork agreeing not to see that lame nigga no more."

LaMonica just looked at him.

"So, are you gonna sign or what?"

"No. I'm not signing nothin'."

"Oh, okay. You grown, huh? Let's see how grown you gonna be in jail."

"Seth looks like we're gonna be taking that ride out to Juvenile after all."

Charlie Jr and his partner drove LaMonica way out past the suburbs of Saginaw Township to the Saginaw County Juvenile Detention Center.

"Last chance, are you willing to sign a paper stating you will not communicate with Bishop Holmes?"

LaMonica responded with a quick "no."

"Fine, then lock up it is."

Charlie Jr walked LaMonica into Juvenile detention. She immediately had to wash her hairstyle out and put on a detention uniform. They promptly escorted her to a cold room to sleep in, made entirely of cement. Her sleeping area was a cement block with a thin "mattress." It reminded her of the preschool nap mats she used as a child. She was given a loosely crocheted blanket for cover. It was like covering up with threads. LaMonica was cold and shivered all night. She just kept thinking, *what is the point of a blanket with holes in it?*

In the morning, a staff member unlocked her cell for breakfast. Everything outside of the cell seemed to move lightning fast. The detainees were allowed 15 minutes to eat breakfast, but LaMonica was unaware of this time limit. It seemed she was to figure out the rules as she went along. Everyone around her was shoveling food into their mouths like it was going out of style.

Since being pregnant, mornings were tricky for LaMonica. She had to choose her food carefully and eat at a slow rate, not to upset her stomach. LaMonica sat, taking slow bites of oatmeal. She had hoped to eat the fruit on her tray next, but the smell of the meat on her plate was threatening to make her nauseous again. She took frequent breaks to settle her stomach, and before she could even get three bites of oatmeal or eat anything else off her plate, the Juvenile Detention staff member announced that breakfast was over, and it was time to move on to the next thing.

They moved on to a round table group discussion and then went back to cells. They released LaMonica once again from lock up for lunch. This time one of the girls warned her.

"You have to eat your food fast or you gonna end up not havin' nothing to eat again. You'd betta get with the program."

As hard as LaMonica tried, she couldn't eat lunch fast without feeling nauseous, so she gave up and just drank the milk that was provided.

After lunch, LaMonica was told that she needed an intake health assessment. They led her to the doctor's office. While examining her, the doctor informed her he had been in contact with her mother and that he knew all about her heart condition. He said her mother was very concerned about her carrying a baby and suggested she terminate the pregnancy.

"Listen, your mom's right. You're too young to have a baby. You should go ahead and have the abortion before it's too late. You're right at the edge of the deadline. I can check you out of here and take you to my office, and we can get it done right away."

LaMonica felt cornered, ambushed, hit from the side. *Like how the heck am I in here getting a health assessment, and the doctor is trying to give me an abortion? And why in the world would the Juvenile Detention doctor be an abortion doctor? This is plain crazy.*

LaMonica gave the doctor a firm "no" and returned to

lock up. Not much had changed inside of her cell. It was still freezing cold, with only holey blankets for cover. It was Summer outside, but it was Winter inside of lock-up. LaMonica guessed it was all the concrete that kept it so cold.

They released her from lockup for outdoor time. Baseball was scheduled for the day's physical activity. All the girls were excited about that. Getting outside would warm everybody up, and it would be nice to be free for a little while. LaMonica saw the girls from breakfast and lunch. As she was gearing up to get on a team, a staff member came running out.

"Wait a minute. I've spoken with Mrs. Powers, the mother of LaMonica Powers, and she doesn't want her playing any sports or exerting herself too much."

LaMonica wasn't surprised about this because Mama had usually stopped her from playing any sort of sports growing up. She said it was dangerous for her heart.

The female staff member told LaMonica just to watch and cheer the other girls on. Quite frankly, LaMonica was fine with it because she sometimes became winded with too much physical activity anyway, especially now that she was pregnant.

When the other girls saw that LaMonica wasn't playing, they got upset. Most of the juvenile inmates were regulars. The staff sort of used the girls to police the newer ones. Sometimes this worked out well, sometimes it didn't.

"Nuh uh, you can't just stand around here and just cheer. You've got to participate, LaMonica, or else you'll lose a privilege."

"They told me not to play baseball."

The female staff member came running over.

"She's not taking part in baseball because she's pregnant."

"Umph. That's not fair; when I was pregnant, I still had to participate in sports here."

"Well, her situation is a little different," the female staff worker responded.

It appeared that a lot of the girls were regulars in juvenile detention. While out in the field, some of the girls began rolling their eyes at LaMonica. They didn't like that she seemed to get special privileges.

At dinner, their frustration with her didn't end.

"Betta hurry up and eat. You got to feed yo' baby, right? Or will she be getting extra time to eat too?"

The staff didn't want the situation to escalate, so they definitely wouldn't be giving LaMonica any extras outside of medical orders.

Try as she might, LaMonica could not eat fast. She was petite and had never been a fast eater to begin with, but now that she was pregnant, it was impossible to just shovel food down her stomach without making herself sick. Thank goodness mashed potatoes were on the menu. She managed to eat a few bites of that and drank half of her milk. Dinner ended quickly in 15 minutes, and now LaMonica was going on 24 hours without eating one full meal.

On the walk back to lock up, the girl who had been upset that LaMonica didn't have to play baseball got really close to her when the female staff member was grabbing supplies and not paying attention.

"You betta watch yo' self. Pretty ain't gonna be able to save you from everythang."

The other girls all gave her a mean look in agreement.

They had a round table discussion before lockup. A lot of the girls revealed they were hurting. Some had had their babies taken away because they were in lock-up. Some had parents on drugs, and some had nowhere to go once they were scheduled for release. It was clear these girls were hurting and at times, looking for someone to take it out on.

As they led LaMonica back to lockup, she dreaded it. She knew she was in for another night of shivering in the cold, and now, to top it off, she was hungry.

After being locked up again in her cell for only about 30 minutes, a female staff member came and let her out.

"We have an emergency meeting with your mother."

They took LaMonica into a conference room where her mother and some other official people were.

"How would you like to get out of here, honey?" an official-looking woman asked.

"Yes. Yes," LaMonica responded.

She was cold, hungry; the doctor was pushing her for an abortion, and all the girls wanted to fight her. *Yes, I sure-enough would like to leave this place immediately.*

"Well, your mother has agreed to some terms, and if you sign this paper, we will release you today."

LaMonica read over the paperwork written on official Family Court letterhead. It stated that she was only to talk to Bishop on the phone one day a week for a set time, and under no circumstances was she to be within 300 feet of him.

At this point, LaMonica was willing to sign anything just to get out of there, so she signed that paper with the quickness. She would just worry about the consequences of not following it later. That's how Mama ended up with the restraining order because LaMonica had signed it to make it out of Juvenile.

Upon release after Mama started waiving her official paper around all the time, B had asked her, "Baby, why would you sign that paper?"

"I needed to get out of there, B. I didn't have a choice."

"Damn baby," Bishop replied.

"I know it's hard in Juvenile. You in a cell in there by yourself. I remember when I was in there. I couldn't get no square or nothin'. I'd take being locked up in the County over Juvenile Detention any day. But damn baby, I really wish you hadn't have cracked and signed that paper. Yo' Mama's gonna make it hard for us."

6

THE POLICE CAN BE YOUR FRIEND

Bishop continued following LaMonica and Mrs. Powers home. He could tell LaMonica was upset based on her movements in the car. Her head was moving erratically. Bishop wasn't sure of what was going on in the car, but it didn't look good. He knew Mrs. Powers would be angry with him for following them home, but he had to make sure LaMonica and his baby were okay.

Something about Mrs. Powers threatening LaMonica with the police set her off even more. She'd had enough of being controlled by threats.

"I didn't do anything today to go to Juvenile for," LaMonica screamed.

"Girl, why are you hollering like a fool? What's wrong with you?"

"You—you are what's wrong with me. You're driving me crazy! You won't let me do anything. I can't wait to get away from you; you're a jailer."

LaMonica continued screaming, and before she knew it, she had said the worst thing a child could say to a mother.

"I hate you."

Mama was tough, but LaMonica knew deep down those words had gotten to her. They pulled into the driveway, and Mama looked at her.

"Look, I'm saving you. That nigga ain't no good, and you're just too blind to see it, LaMonica."

Bishop pulled up in the street in front of the big yellow house on 5th Street. As LaMonica was wobbling out of the car, Mama was running into the house. Bishop got out of his Buick but stayed in the road near the driver's side door.

"You alright, baby?"

"Yeah, I'm fine."

The next thing LaMonica saw was her Mama sprint and jump from the top of the stairs carrying a bat. Bam, bam, bam. She began beating on Bishop's brand-new car. She smashed his hood and dented it up real good. She hit the windshield and cracked it.

"I'm calling the police on you, Mrs. Powers," Bishop lied.

"Go ahead and call the police. They're on their way here anyway, because you ain't have no business taking LaMonica anywhere today."

Bishop was only using calling the police as a scare tactic. He really didn't want any interaction with them, so he sped off before they could come and before Mrs. Powers could hit his windshield one more time and end up shattering it. Mrs. Powers swung her bat behind her neck, with her arms wrapped around each side of it, watching to make sure he left the area.

LaMonica couldn't believe what Mama had just done. This was Bishop's brand-new car. He hadn't had it for even a whole weekend yet.

"Mama, why would you do that to Bishop's caaaar?" she screamed, adding an emphasis on the word car.

"You better watch who you're hollering at LaMonica.

Why would you be out here running around in the streets with that nigga when you know I have a paper that says he shouldn't be anywhere near you? You'd better hope the police don't haul his ass off to jail. Here they come now."

Mrs. Powers ran into the house, placed the bat behind the flowered loveseat on the indoor porch, and then ran back out to greet the police.

"What seems to be the problem here today?" the officer asked.

He also had to ask for Mrs. Powers' name. *Good*, LaMonica thought. *This isn't one of the police officers Mama is friends with.* She might have a shot at talking to him.

"I'm Mrs. Powers, officer, and I have a restraining order against Bishop Holmes being around my daughter. Here it is." Mama pulled the restraining order out for effect.

The officer looked it over. He had never seen anything like it. It wasn't your typical restraining order from County District Court. It was some sort of agreement from the Juvenile Division of Family Court. He would be hesitant to enforce it.

"She left the house with him today while I was at work, and he ain't have no business taking her anywhere. This paper right here states it. He also ain't got no business pullin' up in front of my house. This is my house, and LaMonica is my daughter. I run my house and everything in it." Mrs. Powers felt like she ran everything that happened in and around her house on 5th Street, including LaMonica, not Bishop.

That last statement threw the police officer for a loop. Mrs. Powers seemed a bit controlling to him after that one. He continued getting information from her so he could make his own assessment of the situation.

"How old is this character?" the officer asked.

"He's either 18 or 19," Mrs. Powers replied.

"And your daughter is 16, right?"

"Yes. She's a minor. That's correct."

"When will she be 17?"

"She won't be 17 until next year."

"Do you want her taken in for running away? Because now that she's home, everything appears to be fine."

"No, I don't want her arrested. I just want her to stop running off with that no-count negro, Bishop."

"Okay, well, let me have a talk with her."

The officer instructed Mrs. Powers to go inside of the house so he could speak to LaMonica alone.

"What's going on? Are you safe?"

"Yes. I'm safe. I just don't want to be here anymore."

In all of her frustration, LaMonica just couldn't find the words to express all the reasons she needed to get away from Mama and the big yellow house on 5th Street. She just knew she didn't want to be there anymore. She hadn't really tried to run away that time, but she was thinking about it. She knew it would probably be futile, though, because where would she go? Around the corner to Bishop's house, where Mama would surely come looking for her.

And now, along with everything else, Mama had just beat the mess out of Bishop's brand-new car. These mean acts of Mama's made her want to move in with Bishop all the more.

Without LaMonica explaining it all, the police officer had a good sense of what was going on.

"Listen. I understand you'd prefer to be somewhere else, but if we keep getting calls on you as a runaway, somebody is going to end up taking you in. And I know you don't want to end up back in Juvenile. If you keep going back and forth to Juvenile, then they will petition to become your guardian, and then you'll be stuck locked up and in the system until you're 21."

"If you obey your mom and don't leave without her permission and just wait until you're 17, you can avoid all of this. Legally we cannot accept a runaway report for a 17-year-old.

'I want you to understand your choices very well, LaMonica. If you keep running away or leaving without your mother's permission and being considered a runaway, you could end up locked up until you're 21. If you wait until next year and just move out, no one can touch you."

"Okay, I understand," LaMonica said with a smile on her face.

After speaking one-on-one with the police officer, LaMonica had a new sense of hope. Now that she knew she could definitely move out at 17, she had a firm goal to reach. Mama had pushed her too far. Not only would she leave at 17, but she determined she would say goodbye to living at the big yellow house on 5th Street, THE VERY DAY she turned 17. LaMonica was tired of this, but she would be wise and not end up getting locked up until she was 21.

LaMonica told Bishop and Luchie about the conversation she had with the police officer. After Mama's overbearing tactics, even Luchie couldn't argue with LaMonica's new plan—although she still saw things in Bishop that LaMonica just couldn't see. But overall, she had the support of Luchie and, of course, Bishop. So, this was their new big plan, move out on the day of her 17th birthday no matter what.

7

NESTING

Being at Mama's house felt a little more tolerable now that LaMonica knew for sure she could move out at 17, and all of this was temporary. It kept down a lot of arguments, and LaMonica was able to see once again that even though Mama was heavy-handed in her tactics, at least she did the things she did because she was genuinely concerned about LaMonica's well-being.

Mama had a strong influential personality, and indeed though Mama was often doing what she thought was best for LaMonica, it often didn't feel that way. Luchie, Amalia, and their mom had all had that roundtable discussion with LaMonica back when she first found out she was pregnant, partly based on Mama's influence. Mama's big personality had a lot to do with the type of advice they delivered, even though they were truly concerned for her.

Once LaMonica decided to have the baby, they respected her decision and embraced it wholeheartedly. She spent most of her pregnancy days down the street at Luchie and Amalia's house. And late at night, when Mama was working the bingo on the weekends and not around to look down the street, they were even able to sneak Bishop over.

Amalia would cook good Mexican food for LaMonica. She ate jalapenos almost daily while pregnant. Their brother Martin would play Mexican music on his accordion and entertain everyone. The Marin family made life good for LaMonica while she was waiting to have her baby and move out of Mama's house. Martin would often joke, "You're gonna have to bring the baby down for Mexican music once she's born in order for her to go to sleep."

Luchie and Amalia knew LaMonica's secret plan to move in with Bishop on her 17th birthday. They understood she felt backed into a corner and wanted some control over her own life and the life of her baby, but they also wanted her to be prepared. Luchie would often warn LaMonica of things to look out for once the baby was born.

"Make sure you use cornstarch on the baby and not baby powder. It's safer," Luchie would say.

"Don't worry about name brand or even brand-new clothes for the baby while she's growing. It's okay to have a mix of secondhand clothes and new clothes because babies grow so fast, they'll need a new size almost every month," Amalia advised.

"Don't give the baby the father's last name. You'll have a heck of a time trying to change it later," Luchie warned.

LaMonica followed their advice on everything except that last one. Luchie could see much further up the road than LaMonica could.

Mama never let up on working to keep LaMonica separate from Bishop throughout her pregnancy. After the incident of Mama beating Bishop's car with her bat, LaMonica didn't try to run off with him while Mama was at work anymore. They had to accept the time they had together at school and visits once a week at Luchie's house when Mama was gone from the neighborhood working the bingo.

On the days when LaMonica wasn't at Luchie's house, she would sit on the stairs of the porch. B would often ride down 5th Street on his way to "who knows where." Mostly his usual hood spots. He didn't have a phone at home to call LaMonica and update her with his plans. She would feel so hurt and upset that she couldn't go with him when he would ride by. Bishop would just wave and blow and keep it moving. He didn't want to take a chance on any more problems from Mrs. Powers. Being stuck on those stairs, only able to wave at Bishop as he rode down 5th Street, felt so wrong and restricting. Like she was just one of his regular hood friends that he liked to blow at. She clung to the main objective. They were going to be together when she turned 17. The big goal wouldn't take place until the baby was three months old. That was a lot of time to wait. But LaMonica knew she could do it because who wants to be locked up until they're 21?

LaMonica kept herself happy between going down to Luchie's house for food, family, and fun and shopping with Mama. Once LaMonica was big and showing, Mama really became attached to the idea of having a granddaughter, especially since she favored girls. She and Mama often went on shopping excursions to pick out things for the baby.

During the nesting period, LaMonica gathered everything she needed for the baby. She checked off everything the maternity magazines said a baby needed in a layette which included swaddling blankets, blanket sleepers, t-shirts, onesies, rompers, socks, booties, indoor hats, outdoor hats, no-scratch mittens, and a bunting bag. She washed all the baby's new things in Dreft gentle baby laundry soap to soften the clothes next to the baby's skin.

Some things she bought with her monthly $75 dependent Social Security check and some things Mama bought. As wonderful as a baby-daddy-to-be as Bishop had been on being present for birthing classes and there for her physically, it was a whole different situation on the financial front. Whenever she would ask him for assistance in buying the things the baby needed, he would pull out the same old quote.

"Don't worry; it'll get greater later, baby. One day I'm gonna have a stack of money to give to you and our baby."

In the meantime, while LaMonica waited for that future "stack of money," the baby needed things NOW! LaMonica began pressing B for them. The baby still needed a bed and diapers. After being nearly nine months pregnant, Bishop never came up with a baby bed or diapers. After pressing him to contribute to the things the baby needs, he showed up at Luchie's house one weekend with a pack of baby socks in multiple colors. Luchie worked hard at refraining from commenting on that one. She couldn't believe how naïve LaMonica was when it came to Bishop.

Mama had to end up helping LaMonica get the baby a bassinette because a crib was too expensive without saving for it, and it was getting closer to the time for the baby to be born. LaMonica was insistent that she have everything in preparation. Mama gave LaMonica a baby shower, and she received all the diapers she would need for the baby's first few months, as well as a baby swing, stroller, and car seat. Most of the big stuff Mama had brought to the baby shower. Mama also had a client who lived with her extended family, which included a daughter with a toddler. They gave mama all sorts of barely-worn girl baby clothes for the new baby.

Luchie and Amalia had supplied LaMonica with some baby clothes as well. They had both warned LaMonica that some of the things she insisted on having for the baby were unnecessary. Despite their advice, LaMonica was going to do some things her own way, no matter what. For instance, the beautiful tulle, lace, and ribbons bassinette cover, LaMonica swore the baby couldn't live without. Or the baby walking shoes with bells and ribbon. Luchie had insisted that LaMonica was adding expenses that weren't needed since "duh, the baby can't walk yet." But LaMonica had been adamant that her baby needed to start off in life with proper shoes on. After all the baby items were gathered, LaMonica felt at ease that everything was ready for the baby to be born.

8

THE BIG DAY

Everything seemed to be working in a timely manner. LaMonica and Mama would often be out shopping, and "contractions" would start. She had begun having Braxton Hicks contractions and false labor. Her young body was getting ready for the big event. She and Mama had taken several trips to the hospital, thinking it was time for "the big day." Each time the doctors at the hospital would monitor LaMonica and send her home because she wasn't in actual labor, but it was coming—soon.

When LaMonica had less than a month left before her due date, she began sleeping in the room with Mama. Mrs. Powers had a large bedroom with twin beds that she kept pushed together to make a full-sized bed. Sometimes she rearranged the room and pulled the beds apart. There's something about the third trimester of pregnancy that amps up the maternal instincts and draws a pregnant woman closer to their mother. Besides, despite everything, LaMonica had always felt the safest when she was near Mama. So, when Mama rearranged her room and separated the twin beds, she took that as her opportunity to "move in."

Just in the nick of time, too, because when LaMonica had two weeks left before her due date, she started having contractions in the middle of the night. She followed all the instructions she had received from the doctors when she had Braxton Hicks contractions before—drink lots of water, move around, and finally, if they don't stop, count the minutes in between. Drinking water and moving around didn't stop the contractions, but she and Mama had been to the hospital so many times before they figured it had to be Braxton Hicks. Just in case LaMonica began timing them. They were coming about every 20 minutes consistently.

"Mama, I timed them, and they're coming every 20 minutes."

"How far apart do they have to be for you to definitely be in labor?" Mama asked.

"5 minutes apart."

"Okay, we'll wait until morning and see what's happening."

In the morning, as Mama was getting ready to go to work, LaMonica kept feeling pressure and pain in her back and lower stomach area. The pain was coming off and on. But not more frequently than it did during the night. She wasn't 40 weeks pregnant yet and just kept thinking there was a strong possibility they were still Braxton Hicks. The baby wasn't due for at least another two weeks, and somehow LaMonica had gotten it in her head that she had to be much closer to the due date for this to be real. It was kind of crazy when you think about it because she went running to the hospital every time there was false labor, and now—now that these contractions wouldn't let up, she didn't. Although in the back of her mind, she did remember the warning signs of labor she had learned at school in the Childbirth Class she took with Bishop. After weighing it back and forth, LaMonica decided it was true labor.

"Mama, I keep having the pains off and on, and I think this is real labor. I talked to Luchie about, "true labor" before, and she said it's best to wait until the contractions are closer together before going to the hospital."

"Well, I'm heading off to work. Do you want me to go and get Luchie and bring her down here to sit with you while I'm gone?"

LaMonica looked to Luchie and Amalia for directions on all things "baby." The Marin family were experts in that department. As much as LaMonica loved them, she wanted Bishop by her side right now.

Luchie didn't help me make this baby, LaMonica thought.

"What about B? Mama, can you go around the corner and get B?"

Bishop didn't have a phone. So that would be the only way for him to know what was going on.

"Let me go and see if Luchie's home," Mama replied.

"Sure," LaMonica responded. She knew how Mama felt about Bishop, so Luchie it would be.

The Marins had to prioritize other bills over non-necessities sometimes, so they didn't have a phone at that moment. Mrs. Powers drove down and knocked on the door. It was around 6:45 a.m. It was so early in the morning that no one answered the door for her.

Mama returned home.

"Nobody answered the door LaMonica, and I have to get to work. I can't neglect the morning patients. I'll go to work and see if the office can find a replacement for me for the afternoon."

"Mama, can you please go get Bishop? Please, Mama. What if I'm in labor?" LaMonica whined.

Mama looked at LaMonica. LaMonica could tell she was seriously weighing it.

Mrs. Powers was disgusted by Bishop. She had a restraining order against him, and her pride didn't want her to have to go and knock on Bishop's door for anything. But she was in between a rock and a hard place. She had to be to work, and it probably wasn't a good idea to leave LaMonica alone. So reluctantly, Mrs. Powers went around the corner to Bishop's house.

Boom boom boom. Mrs. Powers was banging on Bishop's door with her fist. Bishop opened the door.

Mrs. Powers didn't waste time on pleasantries.

"LaMonica's at the house in pain and scared she might be in labor. Do you want to come and sit with her while I go to work?"

Mrs. Powers was proud of herself for having such a good tone while having to talk to this fool. She was still upset that Bishop was the one that had put LaMonica in this position in the first place. And who knew what was going to happen to her health-wise when she had this baby.

Bishop was nervous as ever. He had wrecked his brand-new Buick racing and didn't have a car to get LaMonica straight to the hospital. Which is where he felt she needed to be going immediately. He knew he had to humble himself and get a ride around the corner from Mrs. Powers. He wasn't quite sure if that was what she was offering. If need be, he would run like the wind around that corner.

"Can I ride with you, Mrs. Powers?"

"Yes. That's what I came here for. Now hurry up before I'm late for work."

"I'm coming right now, Mrs. Powers. Oh my God, oh my God, oh my God! LaMonica is about to have my baby. Oh my God!"

As soon as LaMonica saw Bishop entering the house, she was so happy. He was utterly nervous.

"Are you okay, baby? We need to get you to a hospital."

"No, I talked to Luchie about this before. My contractions aren't close enough to need to go to the hospital yet. I would just be stuck there for hours, bored. She told me when this happens; I should wait until my contractions are closer." Bishop didn't look convinced.

Mama laughed at the notion that the two of them thought they were ready to be parents. LaMonica was too young to be having a baby anyway. She would need lots of extra help because Bishop was a complete fool. She rolled her eyes at the thought of Bishop as she walked down the hall. Mama had held her composure for as long as she could.

"I'll take you to the hospital when I get off work, LaMonica. Hopefully, I can get a replacement before 3." Mrs. Powers hollered out while closing the door behind her.

Bishop was a nervous wreck. "Baby, we can't wait until your mama gets off work at 3. We've got to get you to a hospital now! Let's call 911 and get you on an ambulance."

Bishop said this as LaMonica was walking around the house gathering cute clothes to put on. She found a pretty pair of pink maternity jeans and a matching shirt and put those on. She left the door open in the bathroom as she was standing in the mirror curling her hair with a curling iron. Every now and again, she would need to take a break for a contraction.

"Baby, I timed you, and now your contractions are 15 minutes apart. You said last night they were 20. Oh my God, you're getting closer, baby. Oh my God!"

Watching LaMonica get primped to go to the hospital made Bishop even more nervous.

"How can you make sure that you have on cute clothes and do your hair at a time like this? We need to get you to the hospital!"

Bishop didn't know what to do with himself, so he called his brother Alonzo and spoke with him and his wife Becky. Becky had just had a baby by Alonzo recently.

"Becky LaMonica is in the bathroom makin' sure she has on the "right" outfit and doin' her hair at a time like this. I can't believe this girl. She should be going to the emergency right now. We should be calling the ambulance. I can't even sway her."

"Calm down, B," Becky told Bishop.

"She's probably got a lot of time. When was the last contraction?"

"Baby, when was the last time you had a pain?"

"About 15 minutes ago. But here comes another one," LaMonica replied.

"Oh yeah, you can calm down, Bishop. 15 minutes apart, you guys have plenty of time. Don't worry."

"Yeah, they're 15 minutes apart, but they're getting closer. She started off at 20 minutes apart. This is real labor."

"It's going to be okay, B. Trust me, I just had your nephew."

By noon LaMonica's pains had gotten stronger. She went to the bathroom and saw what's called "the bloody show." LaMonica and Bishop had both learned about "the bloody show" during Childbirth Class at school. It's when the mucous plug comes out when a woman's body is getting closer to giving birth. Bishop hadn't been paying that part much attention in class, but LaMonica had. Now she knew it was definitely time to go to the hospital.

"Bishop, I just had my 'bloody show,' and my mucous plug just came out."

The look on LaMonica's face told him things were getting serious now.

Bishop frantically called Becky back.

"Becky, she just had her bloody show! Oh my goodness!"

"B has her water broken yet?"

"Baby, your water hasn't broke yet, has it?"

"No, B, I don't think so," LaMonica answered.

Mrs. Powers clicked in on the phone. "Let me talk to LaMonica."

Bishop was pacing the living room floor while LaMonica was talking with Mama.

"I was just calling to check on you. How are you doing, LaMonica?"

"I think I should go to the hospital, Mama. I just had my 'bloody show,' and the contractions are getting closer."

"Okay, I'm on my way. I have already seen my morning clients, and I let the office know what's going on. They're going to send a replacement for me for the rest of my clients, so I'm on my way."

"She's coming, Bishop."

"Thank God." Bishop was relieved.

Mama made it and took LaMonica and Bishop to the hospital. The hospital verified that LaMonica was, in fact, in the early stages of labor and placed her in a special labor and delivery room called LDRP. LDRP stood for labor, delivery, recovery, and post-partum. Instead of a mother having to be carted from room to room through each stage of giving birth, these rooms were equipped to handle each stage all in one room. The LDRP rooms were beautiful. They were upgraded to look almost like hotel rooms. LaMonica had found out about them while attending Child Birthing classes at Ruben Daniels. She always wanted the best of everything if she could obtain it. LaMonica was one of the first few people to know about these rooms, so everyone who visited her was impressed.

After a couple of hours of labor, Mama said she would go by Luchie's house and let her know what was going on. LaMonica was fine because Bishop was right by her side the whole time. He would try to keep her distracted as the contraction monitor lines would go up and up.

"You're doing good, baby. They're going down. Just breathe."

Mama came back and said Luchie would be coming to visit soon. She stayed with Bishop and LaMonica for quite a few hours. Each time the contraction monitor showed contractions getting stronger and longer, Bishop would lie and say, "Don't worry, baby, they're on their way down. It's about to be over soon."

Mrs. Powers would blurt out. "No, they're not! Those contractions are going up and up on that monitor."

Bishop couldn't believe Mrs. Powers. He was trying to keep LaMonica calm and in good spirits.

"You know if you want to take a break and go get somethin' to eat, you can, Mrs. Powers. I'll be right here."

Mrs. Powers took Bishop up on that offer and went down to the cafeteria.

"Man, I can't believe yo' Mama. Why would she tell you it's getting worse? It's like she wants to scare you or somethin'?"

Bishop already didn't like that Mrs. Powers had kept LaMonica informed of all sorts of stories of people dying while giving birth—throughout her pregnancy. He welcomed a breather from her.

9

MONICA

As soon as Mrs. Powers left for the cafeteria, Bishop informed LaMonica he had to step out for a minute. It had been all day. He had gone as long as he could without a cigarette.

"Baby, I need to run outside and smoke me a square. But I'll be back in a minute."

"Okay," LaMonica replied.

It was the first time she had been completely alone since being in labor, and wouldn't you know it, that's when her labor pains became more intense.

"Ay yay yah."

LaMonica could be heard down the halls. She tried the breathing techniques she had learned from Child Birthing Class, but nothing seemed to help.

"Ahhhhhhhhh!"

LaMonica's painful moans were getting louder and louder.

A nurse came in.

"Hey. Somebody's in pain. Are you in here all by yourself?"

"Yes. My boyfriend went on a smoke break, and my mom's in the cafeteria."

"Alright, well, let's see what we can do for your pain. Let me check your contractions first."

LaMonica watched the nurse as she checked the printed sheet from the contraction monitor.

"Yes. They're getting pretty strong. Let me go get the doctor and see what we can give you for pain."

LaMonica had been in labor for hours now, but the pain had just now become unbearable. As the nurse was leaving, another contraction started up, and LaMonica began moaning again. Bishop came back into the room and met the nurse.

"Baby, are you okay?"

LaMonica didn't respond; she just had a painful look on her face.

"Nurse, is she okay? She looks like she's in a lot of pain."

"Yes, I'm going to get the doctor to get her something for pain."

The doctor came in and checked LaMonica's cervix.

"You're dilated to 6, hun. If you're going to get an epidural, you'll have to get one now. Once your cervix dilates close to 8, we can't administer it."

The doctor began explaining that the epidural would numb LaMonica's lower half of her body. She would no longer feel pain but pressure during labor. LaMonica was very familiar with an epidural from her training in Child-birth Class at Ruben Daniels.

"So, are we moving forward with the epidural?" the doctor asked.

"Yes. I'm ready," LaMonica replied.

Bishop looked nervous as ever.

"Alright, we're going to get the Anesthesiologist in here."

The Anesthesiologist arrived, and he said Bishop could stay for the procedure. As the nurse gave LaMonica IV fluids and prepped her, she invited Bishop to witness the Anesthesiologist place the needle in her back.

Bishop watched as they inserted the entire 8-centimeter needle into LaMonica's back. He complained of Mrs. Powers making LaMonica nervous earlier, but he couldn't help but wince with commentary.

"Ohhh, that needle is long. Oh, my goodness! Whew!"

LaMonica had remained perfectly still. She had heard rumors that if you moved at all during the epidural, you could end up paralyzed, so no matter how bad Bishop was making the whole process sound, she wasn't going to speak or move one inch until that needle was out of her back.

In the meantime, Mama had returned from the cafeteria and was out in the hallway. The staff wouldn't let her in until the procedure was complete.

"What do you mean I can't go in there? Who authorized my daughter to have an epidural anyway? She's a minor ya'll are supposed to get my permission before you do any procedures on her. She has a heart issue, and she can't take everything that everybody else can take?"

"Mrs. Powers, your daughter was in pain while you were away, and so we gave her something for it. She is the patient, after all."

"Will this affect her heart?"

"No ma'am. An epidural has very few side effects, and we are monitoring her closely. In all honesty, with her pain level being reduced by the epidural—if anything, I would think it's reducing the stress on her heart."

"You think?" Mrs. Powers said. Ella Mae Powers was still upset that the hospital had administered such a significant drug to a 16-year-old without her permission.

Finally, the epidural procedure was over, and Mrs. Powers was let back into the LDRP suite. LaMonica was finally out of pain and only felt pressure with each contraction. The nurse remained in the room, checking LaMonica's charts and observing Mrs. Powers' reaction.

"How you feelin'?" Mama asked LaMonica.

"Better now that I have this epidural."

"Well, they didn't have no business giving you somethin' like that when I wasn't here."

"Mama, the pain had gotten worse when you left."

"She was in an extreme amount of pain, ma'am. I heard her from down the hall," the nurse added.

"Someone should have come and gotten me from the cafeteria," Mrs. Powers said while looking at Bishop.

"Well, it looks like you'll get to see that grandbaby soon. Any names picked out?" the nurse said while trying to change the subject and de-escalate the situation.

It worked. Mrs. Powers instantly got excited at the thought of being able to help pick out her granddaughter's name.

"Oh yes, my friend who works with me gave me a list of names for us to go over."

"Okay, let's look at them, Mama." LaMonica and Bishop already had a first name picked out, but she hadn't decided on a middle name. She would let Mama help with that.

"You guys have fun picking out those names," the nurse said. Now that she knew things were on a good note, she left the family alone to pick out names and wait for the baby's delivery.

"This is the list that Jean gave me," Mama said.

Bishop's favorite aunt—Aunt Frieda, had already asked LaMonica to name the baby Monica.

"I just love that name, Monica, LaMonica. It sounds so

much like yours, and I just know she's going to be such a beautiful baby. Please name her after you."

LaMonica loved Aunt Frieda. She was more like a grand-mother to LaMonica and Bishop than an aunt. She was always doing them special favors. If there was anything Aunt Frieda wanted LaMonica to do, she would do it, plus she just had such a beautiful heart.

"I'm going to name the baby Monica Mama. But I still need a middle name."

Mama was fine with the first name because it was so close to LaMonica's name. Never would she have guessed that it was actually Bishop's family that wanted her to have that name.

LaMonica read over the list of names from Mama's friend Jean.

"Dawn, Brianna, Cheyenne, Summer, Autumn, Mercedes, and Deja."

"Well, I'm cool with whatever you pick for the middle name as long as her name is Monica," Bishop said while kicking back and watching TV. He would just let Mrs. Powers and LaMonica do their thang on that one.

"Hmmm. Dawn stands out among all the other names to me, but I'm not sure. I definitely don't like Brianna. It just doesn't stand out to me. Cheyenne sounds like a cowgirl from the country. Summer and Autumn don't fit the season, and I'm definitely not naming my baby Winter, although I read this book once called, The Coldest Winter Ever. The main character's name was Winter—"

Bishop shot LaMonica a look that said, "I know you can't be seriously thinking this name over."

"Okay, no, definitely not Winter."

"Hmmm, Mercedes, Mercedes. I like the name Mercedes, but I know a lot of girls with that name too."

"Yeah, and they're all snotty too," Bishop said.

"I thought you didn't care about the middle name?"

"Oh, I don't, really. I'm just sayin' though."

"What about the last one on the list—Deja?" Mama asked.

"No, I don't like that one either. Sounds too hood."

"Sounds like a strip club," Bishop added.

"Well, Jean said she was gonna give me some more names when her daughter gets home. We'll look at those too."

"Alright, Mama."

So, no middle name was decided yet.

It got later into the evening, and LaMonica's contractions were getting stronger and stronger, according to the charts. LaMonica didn't pay it much mind, though, since she had the epidural.

Bishop, Mama, and LaMonica began watching comedy shows on TV. That's when Luchie and their other friend Camila walked in.

"Girl, how are you up here laughing at a TV show? You should be screaming in pain by now."

"Hey, Luchie." LaMonica and Luchie hugged.

"They gave me an epidural, girl. I'm pretty much numb on the lower half of my body. I only feel pressure when the contractions come."

"I was looking forward to coming in here messing with you while you were in horrible pain. This is not fair. How far are you dilated?"

"The last time they checked, I was around 8 centimeters."

"What no way. You're almost there, and you're not screaming in pain. I can't believe this. I was hollering, screaming, and crying by now with Chara. This is so not fair."

It's not that Luchie necessarily wanted LaMonica to suffer, but she knew from experience that it was that pain that deterred her from having other children too fast.

"Well, at least we can torture you with food. Bishop and Mrs. Powers, have you eaten yet?"

"Oh yes, thank you. I grabbed something earlier from the cafeteria," Mrs. Powers said.

"What about you, B?"

"Nawl. The last time I left LaMonica alone, she was in extreme pain and ended up getting a shot in her back. I can't leave now that it's this close. I don't want to miss nothin'."

"Well, check this out; I've got some tamales in my bag. You want some?"

"Yeah, I'll take a couple."

"LaMonica, you can't have anything to eat, so you just sit over there and eat your ice chips, okay."

LaMonica knew that Luchie was just messing with her. Let them have their fun. But at the same time, she looked at Bishop like he'd better not eat that tamale while she was stuck eating only ice chips.

Bishop took one look at LaMonica, "Yeah, I'm just gonna wrap em up and save them for later."

"Why because LaMonica can't eat?" Luchie asked.

Bishop smirked. "I'm glad ya'll are here, though. I'm gonna run outside and smoke a square real quick.

'I'll be right back, baby."

Bishop kissed LaMonica on the cheek and left the hospital room.

Luchie had seen so many births - Amalia and her sister Genevieve's births of her nieces and nephews, even her mother's birth of her baby brother Emiliano. Her family knew a lot about having babies and taking care of them. But epidurals were new. Never in her life had Luchie seen a woman in active labor and dilated to 8cm casually laugh, talk, and joke. *What was this craziness?*

"So, they put medicine in your spine?" Luchie asked.

"Yes," LaMonica replied.

"I hope that doesn't give you problems with your back later in life."

"I said the same thing," Mama added.

They were both starting to make LaMonica nervous. Camila looked worried as well.

LaMonica's pulse began to rise. Bishop came back in from his smoke break. With one look at LaMonica's face, he knew something was wrong.

"What's wrong, baby?"

"Luchie and Mama said I might need to worry about back problems from the epidural shot."

Bishop couldn't believe this. He had left LaMonica with Mrs. Powers for a few minutes, and there she was, scaring her again.

"You don't have to worry about that. The doctor already said there weren't those kinds of risks with it. Besides, they wouldna' gave it to you if that was the case. These people don't want to be sued."

"Yeah, you're right, and besides, they said it was a good option in class."

"Don't let that stuff worry you, baby," Bishop said.

Luchie stayed and joked around with everyone for a little while. She had to leave after an hour or two because she had to get back home to her daughter. Camila stayed, which was interesting because she and LaMonica weren't nearly as close as LaMonica and Luchie. Secretly Camila had just found out she was pregnant herself and wanted to see what the whole ordeal of having a baby was about.

LaMonica began to feel more intense pressure, and the

contractions were coming faster and faster. She wasn't in pain, but something in her body was definitely different. Mama and B noticed too. When the nurse came in, they both mentioned this to her.

"Alright, let me get a doctor in here to check her cervix."

The doctor came in and announced it was near time for the delivery. They wanted the room clear, and only one other person could stay with LaMonica.

"Who do you want in here with you during the delivery, hun?" the nurse asked.

"Bishop. I want my boyfriend Bishop here with me."

Mrs. Powers immediately began to get upset.

"LaMonica is a minor. I need to be in here with her."

"Mrs. Powers, even though LaMonica is a minor, she still has the right to choose who she wants in the delivery room with her," the nurse informed Mrs. Powers.

This put Mrs. Powers on high alert. She was losing control of the situation. What if things went wrong during delivery and she wasn't there? So, she reverted back to her trusty tried and true restraining order paper. It had worked at Ruben Daniels school to separate LaMonica from Bishop. It had certainly achieved her purpose at LaMonica's ultrasound appointment when Bishop was there, and he didn't have no business being there. And it would work today. It just had to.

Mrs. Powers reached in her purse and pulled out her secret weapon, the Juvenile Division of Family Court's official restraining order against Bishop Holmes.

"Look here; I have a restraining order against him. He's not allowed to be around her."

The nurse was baffled that suddenly Mrs. Powers didn't want Bishop around LaMonica when he had been there all day.

"I'm going to go get scrubbed up while you sort this out," the doctor told the nurse."

The nurse and the staff knew full well that Bishop had, in fact, come to the hospital with LaMonica and her mother. Mrs. Powers hadn't had any issue with him being around LaMonica up until the point where she couldn't get her way. This was a power play.

Two more staff members came into the room while the nurse spoke with Mama. LaMonica was dilated to 9cm and time was of the essence. The nurse knew that to de-escalate the situation; she would have to handle this situation delicately, so she chose her words carefully.

"Mrs. Powers, it's important for the father to witness the mother giving birth, especially when the mother is a teenager. We've found that it helps to deter more teenage pregnancies when they see how much pain she's in. We try to involve the fathers as much as we can so that they see everything the mother goes through, and hopefully, it will help them make better-informed decisions to not continue having teenage pregnancies."

The nurse had spoken the magic words. That was it. That was enough to convince Mrs. Powers to let Bishop stay and not use her paperwork against him. If witnessing LaMonica give birth would ensure she wouldn't have more babies with him, then heck yes, she would leave and let him be there.

Of course, a part of her was hurt from missing the birth. The nurse saw it and encouraged her.

"You can wait right here on the floor, and as soon as the baby is born, and the doctor looks her over, I'll run and get you. I know you're anxious to see that grandbaby." Camila followed Mrs. Powers to the waiting room.

And so, against restraining orders and all odds, Bishop

remained there with LaMonica and saw his baby being born. The moment Monica entered the world, Bishop followed her everywhere she went. They plopped the baby on top of LaMonica, and he cut the cord. LaMonica noted that her hair was wet from blood and fluid, and it was curly. She only had a chance to glance at the baby because they were moving her around so much.

Bishop followed the staff and his baby as they placed Monica in the incubator and cleaned her up. When they said they had to take the baby to the nursery to dress her and give further tests, he followed them, watching through the window. Bishop and LaMonica had seen a movie on TV where babies were switched, and he wasn't taking any chances. He studied Monica's face and watched as they put on her arm bands. He knew his baby already.

Bishop returned to LaMonica's side.

"You did so good, baby."

The nurse told them the baby was 6lbs 5oz. LaMonica already knew from Luchie that as babies go, that was a small baby.

"She's small, isn't she?" LaMonica asked the nurse, a little worried.

"She's about right. Look at you two; you're both small people."

LaMonica felt at ease then.

10

BENTLEY

B ishop was on a high. He had seen his baby being born. He had almost missed that chance in so many ways. Back when LaMonica was about 6 months pregnant, he had been in a car accident. His cousin Gary had tried to kill them both in a murder-suicide. They were riding together one night, and Gary, a corporate executive, was hopped up on cocaine. He had recently suffered a mental breakdown and was released from a psych ward.

As they were riding, Gary took them way out in the woods. He suddenly started driving faster and faster near a cliff. Then he declared – "I'm ready to die cuz, and I'm gonna take you with me."

Bishop saw his life flash before his eyes and the last thought he had before passing out from the impact was, *I'm not ever gonna see my baby.*

He had called up to Ruben Daniels and told LaMonica what happened. She walked to the hospital all the way from school. When she got there, the doctor said, "I'm glad you're here. All he's been saying is 'I need to see my woman. I need to see my woman'."

Bishop didn't press charges against his cousin at the request of his family. His mom had reasoned with him.

"You know that boy needs mental help, B. Don't get him locked up."

Bishop agreed he wouldn't press charges because his mom asked him not to; besides, he didn't like dealing with the police anyway. He would deal with Gary in his own way and at just the right time.

~

*B*ishop called his mother to let her know that Monica was here.

"Oooh, I'm so excited, B. I'm on my way!" Anna exclaimed.

The hospital staff finished dressing and testing the baby and brought her back into the room. LaMonica held her. She was absolutely beautiful. All she could do was stare at her. She had the perfect face, the perfect eyes, nose, everything. But her hair was now straight.

"Bishop, why is this baby's hair straight? The baby had curly hair when I had her."

"Baby, that's our baby. I followed them and watched everything they did. Her hair is just like yours, curly when wet and straight when dry, I guess."

They both laughed. LaMonica was just a new anxious mom.

Bishop and LaMonica took turns holding the baby. Then the nurse went into the waiting room and got Mrs. Powers and Camila.

Mama was overjoyed at seeing her new grandbaby. She held her and remarked on how beautiful she was.

"Yes, she's beautiful. She's gonna be fine," Bishop remarked.

Anna made it to the hospital in a flash. She must have been speed racing.

"Oooh, look at her. Look at grandmama's new suga'. Ohhh, she's such a doll."

Camila just observed everything. Between those two grandmas, she couldn't get in to actually hold the baby. But she had learned a lot for when it was her time. Camila's mom came and picked her up, and she and LaMonica said their goodbyes.

Eventually, everyone left for the night, and it was just Bishop and LaMonica. Bishop and LaMonica took turns taking care of Monica before night fell. LaMonica's white cell count was up after the delivery, and the doctors and nurses wanted her to rest. When the baby cried in the middle of the night, Bishop grabbed her and held her all night long as he slept in a rocking chair.

When Mama returned in the morning, she was furious that Bishop was asleep in the chair with the baby.

"Did you sleep all night in the chair holding that baby?"

"Yes," Bishop replied.

"That's not safe. You could've dropped her," Mama said.

"Oh, nawl. Ain't no way I'm gonna drop my baby. She was safe in my arms all night."

"Baby, I'm gonna step outside and go smoke me a square. I'll be back."

Bishop was trying his best to respect Mrs. Powers, so he thought it was best he stepped outside.

"LaMonica, don't you let him do that again. That's dangerous letting him hold that baby all night."

LaMonica just looked at Mama without responding.

Maybe she was right. She wouldn't let Bishop do that again, but he was just trying to bond with his baby.

Little did LaMonica know that this was just a preview of Mama trying to assume control of her child way up the road. Even though she had fought her tooth and nail to have an abortion, her objectives would change.

Mama seemed so excited about the baby. She came in, washed her hands, and wanted to hold her right away.

The nurse informed them that the clerk would be in soon to fill out the official birth certificate.

"Let's call Jean. Her daughter should be home now with some more baby names."

"Okay, Mama." LaMonica was excited about that.

Mama got on the phone and started calling out the names that Jean's daughter had given her. LaMonica wrote them down as she called each one out.

"Brooke, Sierra, Diamond, Shanice, Bentley," Mama called out.

"Okay, they're looking for her to fill out the birth certificate soon. I'll call you back and let you know what we come up with," Mama told Jean.

"Brooke, no. Sierra sounds interesting, but I don't know what that means. Diamond and Shanice too hood, but Bentley. I like Bentley. You don't hear it a lot. Bentley it is."

When the clerk came, LaMonica gave them Monica's full name. "Monica Bentley Holmes."

"Holmes?" Mama didn't like the sound of that.

"You're naming the baby's last name Holmes?"

"Yes, Mama, I can't name her after me. I'm named after your late husband, Richard Powers Sr. and I never even knew him. She wouldn't be connected to anybody with that name."

"Well, I have the name Powers, and you do too; we're connected."

"Mama, I'm going to get married one day, and Powers won't be my last name. I want Monica's last name to be Holmes."

"Can people do that?" Mrs. Powers directed her question to the clerk.

"Can they name the baby after the father even if they aren't married?"

"Honestly, ma'am, legally, you can name a child any last name you want to. It doesn't even have to be the mother or father's last name."

"Wow, I didn't know that," Mama said.

"Is the father here?" the clerk asked.

"Yes, he's here. He just took a break," LaMonica said.

"I see here you wrote you are single. We can still add him to the birth certificate if he fills out a Paternity Affidavit."

"Okay, good, he wants to be on the birth certificate," LaMonica replied.

"Excellent, well, I'm just going to leave this paperwork here for him to sign, and when the father completes the affidavit, we'll make sure to get him added to the birth certificate. Just hit the call light when you're done."

LaMonica filled out her part of the paperwork with the baby's official name, Monica Bentley Holmes. When Bishop came back in, she gave him the news.

"I filled out the baby's birth certificate. The clerk said you can be added to her birth certificate if you fill out this affidavit."

Bishop immediately began filling out the paperwork. He purposely put his social security number down one digit off. He was thinking long-term in case somebody tried to come after him for child support later on down the road. LaMonica was oblivious to this, though. He then read across the birth certificate application, Monica's full name. Monica *Bentley* Holmes.

"Bentley? Bentley?"

"That's Monica's middle name, B."

"So, you're tellin' me you named my daughter after a car?"

"I like it. It's a unique name Bishop."

"Bentley umph."

Bishop looked disgusted. He finished filling out the paperwork, and LaMonica pushed the call light for the clerk to come take it. They didn't check social security numbers for Paternity Affidavits in those days, so Bishop's off-digit social security number would fly under the radar.

So, Monica Bentley Holmes, daughter of Bishop Holmes and LaMonica Powers, it was.

11

TEENAGE PLANS

A fter LaMonica gave birth to Monica, Mama went right back to her original game plan. She didn't want B anywhere near her house most of the time; every now and again, she would change her mind and then go right back to banning him again and threatening him with the police.

Bishop's mother, Anna, worked in a high official job in Detroit. After everything she had seen from Mrs. Powers, she knew that once LaMonica moved in with Bishop, Mrs. Powers would be giving them hell. So, she put plans in motion to have her job transferred by the time LaMonica was old enough to move out. That way, she could be there at the drop of a dime when the drama began.

On one occasion, when LaMonica had somehow snook out with Bishop to visit Anna, she gave her some advice.

"Yo' Mama is something else, honey. She seems a bit controlling. Kicking B out of the ultrasound appointment and trying to kick him out of the delivery- whooh. You have to sneak to even let Monica be around her own people. After everything I've seen, it would probably be in your best interest to stop letting her know about your plans."

LaMonica agreed. There were only three months left before she would turn 17. Mama wasn't letting up and still making her feel caged even though she herself was now a parent. There wasn't much she wanted to do – just take care of her own baby and let her see her father and his family sometimes.

Mama had slipped up and complained about Bishop and his side of the family to Uncle Charlie. Up until that point, he had no idea how his sister had been handling the situation.

"LaMonica keeps sneakin' out of this house with that nigga Bishop. I'm gonna have him locked up sooner or later; just you watch, brother."

"Now Ella Mae, LaMonica has had a baby by him now. There ain't no use in trying to keep her away from him at this point. The damage has been done. If he wants to stay and be a father, you shouldn't try to separate them."

Mama respected her brother, so she listened to him for the moment. She began letting LaMonica talk to Bishop on the phone more than the allotted one day a week (according to the Family Court restraining order). Mama would listen in on their conversations, though.

LaMonica told Bishop everything all the time, where she had been for the day, what plans she had. Everything.

"I took the baby down to the WIC office for her formula coupons today Bishop. They measured her growth too. They said she's a little on the short side, but her weight is good."

"Oh, that's good, baby. Yeah, she's probably gonna be short like her Mama."

"Ha ha," Bishop and LaMonica would both laugh.

Mama couldn't stand their conversations. Now that

LaMonica was allowed to talk to Bishop on the phone every evening (thanks to Uncle Charlie), she ran with excitement to answer it whenever it rang.

"I guess you've got to report to yo' nigga," Mama would say in disgust.

LaMonica planned on going back to Ruben Daniels to complete her high school diploma after 3-6 weeks of post-partum. When she told Bishop this, he was adamant that he didn't want his baby in that daycare inside the school.

"There's way too many babies in there, crawling around not getting any attention. Nawl, my baby, ain't goin' in there. See because if she gets hurt, I'm goin' to prison."

This threw LaMonica off her plan because Bishop had never said anything about this before. But honestly, her friend Jaqueline had her baby in there, and often times her screw-back diamond earrings would be missing, and her formula bottle would sometimes be old and stale. They did have a lot of babies crawling around in there on that floor in comparison to staff. *And what if someone stepped on Monica?*

Even though Mama was semi-retired, she still worked during the day. Bishop never made himself available to watch the baby during the day, so LaMonica dropped out of high school full time and enrolled in night classes.

General Assistance (GA) welfare benefits were canceled for adults without children in the State of Michigan, and Bishop stopped attending Ruben Daniels full time as well. He hustled up on a car and enrolled in night classes with LaMonica. Mama would watch Monica for a couple of hours while LaMonica went to limited night classes with Bishop during the week.

Mama was okay with Bishop picking LaMonica up for high school classes. Still, when they would stay an hour over just to have time alone, she began to complain.

"I don't want that nigga in my driveway LaMonica."

LaMonica knew that anytime Mama wanted to, she could pull out her trusty restraining order paper. She ended up giving up on school altogether. Besides, attending Ruben Daniels at night just wasn't the same. The classes seemed much more accelerated. The focus was no longer on Child Development and Child Care. And she just didn't feel motivated enough to leave her baby every night and continue.

Mama taking Uncle Charlie's advice to allow Bishop in LaMonica, and Monica's lives was short-lived. She would change her mind back and forth on Bishop picking LaMonica and the baby up, but under no circumstances did she want Bishop in her house. Sometimes LaMonica would sneak him in to see the baby when she was at work. Sometimes, Bishop would pick LaMonica and the baby up and take them to visit with his Aunt Frieda.

Days seemed to fly by. LaMonica was busier than she'd ever been before. Every two hours, she was feeding the baby and changing the baby. In the morning, she was dressing and bathing her. She was singing to her, dancing with her, reading to her. Before she knew it, it was time to go to bed, get up, and do it all over again the next day.

LaMonica bought all the things she needed month to month for the baby with her dependent $75 a month Social Security check. For anything that that didn't cover, Mama would pitch in and get it. Mama also bought baby Monica a new frilly dress every month from the mall. Bishop never did kick in financially on any of the baby's needs. He still had that same saying though, "It'll get greater later, baby."

LaMonica was holding out for later with Bishop. In the meantime, her birthday month rolled around. It was almost time for her to move out, and Mama still had no idea. Mama had decided to completely retire from her main job and collect her full Social Security check. She would just be working security on the weekends from now on and helping one or two clients during the week. LaMonica heard her on the phone one day talking to her good friend Jean.

"I know, honey. I can't wait to retire. I'm gonna be so happy being here with the baby every day."

LaMonica felt bad because, Mama would in fact, not be there with the baby every day because she would be gone.

~

The night before LaMonica's 17th birthday, Luchie had a girls' night planned for the two of them. LaMonica and Luchie were upstairs in Luchie's room giggling like happy young girls while painting each other's toenails and trying on lingerie. They were telling each other funny stories from the past and even laughing about old boyfriends. Mama was babysitting the baby tonight with no idea that LaMonica planned on leaving her home for good the following day.

Out of nowhere, while they were running around in lingerie and giggling, Luchie and LaMonica saw someone on the roof.

"Awe shoot, girl, I think I just saw somebody moving around on the roof!" Luchie exclaimed.

LaMonica and Luchie ran to the window. There definitely someone out there in the night on the rooftop.

"I've got a bat under the bed. Hurry up and grab it, LaMonica."

LaMonica grabbed the bat and passed it to Luchie. That's when the intruder came from the shadows of the rooftop and revealed himself.

"Oh my goodness, Luchie, it's B!"

Luchie covered her mouth with her hand. She almost cussed him out.

LaMonica began releasing a slow smile that got wider and wider as she ran to the window to open it for Bishop.

"Luchie, it's stuck. I don't know how to open it," LaMonica whined.

Reluctantly Luchie raised the window to see what Bishop wanted.

He climbed through the window, holding a bottle of gin.

"Baby, I'm just so excited about tomorrow. I had to come by and see you. Tomorrow's the big day."

Staring deep into LaMonica's eyes, Bishop repeated, "I couldn't wait, baby, I had to come and see you."

Bishop had been sitting on top of Luchie's rooftop, watching the both of them laughing and running around in lingerie with amusement while he nursed a bottle of gin. After his embrace with LaMonica, he cracked a joke about it.

"Yeah y'all, I was like, I've got to go around here and see my woman. Man, I was so surprised to see you two teeny-boppers running around in lingerie, hahaha."

Of course, Bishop knew where LaMonica would be because she kept him informed of her every move, but he had no idea what a girls' night looked like until he got there.

Luchie was thoroughly aggravated. *Why would B do this when he was gonna have LaMonica all to himself starting tomorrow? Couldn't he allow LaMonica to have a girls' night without him interfering?*

"Yeah, well, we're trying to have a girls' night. No dudes allowed," Luchie snapped at Bishop.

LaMonica was just happy to see B. She was pleased that Bishop cared so much about her. She didn't get what Luchie was so upset about.

Luchie felt violated. Here Bishop was violating their girls' night while they were running around giggling in lingerie.

"Bishop LaMonica is moving in with you tomorrow. Let me have time with my friend today."

"Okay, I'll let you ladies have girls' night. You're all mine, tomorrow, baby," Bishop said as he kissed LaMonica and climbed back down off the roof.

Luchie rolled her eyes and blew her breath.

"That was some BS, LaMonica."

"What?" LaMonica asked.

"Bishop climbing up here on the roof all in the window while we're trying to have girls' night. He could've waited. You're already moving around there, and he's gonna have you all the time."

Luchie could see the controlling ways in Bishop. LaMonica couldn't see it. All she could see was how much he cared about her.

12

300 FEET

LaMonica had been storing clothes under her bed for weeks now, just like she did that night she and Luchie and Juan all ran away together. On the morning of her birthday, she knew she would have to act fast. All of Monica's things were easy to get to because she had them neatly stored in her baby drawers.

Even though Mama had retired from being an official Home Health Aide with the company she worked for, she still agreed to see a couple of clients on the side. It just wasn't like her to not work. As luck would have it, LaMonica's 17th birthday was on a Saturday, and Mama was working. Mama had talked with her that morning and asked her what she wanted for her birthday.

"What do you want for your birthday LaMonica? We can run by the mall and grab you something after I get out of work? Do you still want those boots?"

Mama had bought LaMonica a long leather trench coat for Christmas. LaMonica had remarked she wouldn't mind having the leather boots to match. The boots alone were

$100, so of course, Mama couldn't buy both at the same time.

"We'll see what happens for your birthday," she had said.

LaMonica felt so guilty. How could she agree to have Mama go buy her leather boots when she was moving out today? She already knew moving out with the baby was gonna really make Mama mad. But if she said or did anything out of the ordinary, it would make her suspicious, and then Mama might sneak back home and try to block her from moving out. She would have to make sure things appeared to be normal.

"Sure, Mama. That'll be nice. Thank you."

"Okay, well, I should be done with my client around 3 today. So, you and the baby be ready."

"Alright, we will," LaMonica lied.

As soon as Bishop was satisfied Mama was gone, he pulled into the driveway. He and LaMonica began fervently putting all of her and the baby's things in the car. Mama's trusty neighbors were watching through the windows too. But this time no matter what they reported, nothing could be done about it. She was 17 now!

LaMonica, Bishop, and Monica made it around the corner to Bishop's house. LaMonica hadn't taken any big stuff from Mama's house, only the things that were hers. She had always heard Mama say that legally anything anyone gives you as a gift is yours to keep. So, she kept all of her and Monica's "gifts."

At 3p.m. Mrs. Powers came home to an empty house. Not only were LaMonica and the baby gone, but so were all of their things. *So, she's moved out.* Things had been going well with her and LaMonica, so Mrs. Powers was hurt, surprised, and disgusted.

She bolted outside for the car. Ginnie Lee, the next-door neighbor, hollered at her.

"Hey, Mrs. Powers. I saw that boyfriend of LaMonica's pull up. They were moving stuff out quickly. I think she's gone around that corner to stay with him."

"Yeah, that's probably where she is. I'm going around there to check now."

"Well, keep a cool head. Sometimes we can make it worse when we try to tell these young folks what to do. You know they already think they know everythang."

"Yeah." Mrs. Powers just listened and was taking in what Ginnie Lee said.

"You know I've got some grown ones over here. Sometimes you just have to let them bump their heads a little bit so they can learn."

Mama had Ginnie Lee's words on her mind as she was driving around the corner to Bishop's house on Norman Street. She decided she didn't want to push LaMonica away. Her adopted daughter Deb had left for Mississippi when LaMonica was a baby, and no one had seen or heard from her until about 5 years ago. LaMonica was the baby out of Richard and Deb. She was the one that she was the closest to. And now that she had had Monica, Mama had fallen in love with her too. She couldn't lose them both. She was mulling these thoughts around as she pulled into Bishop's driveway. Mrs. Powers walked onto Bishop's porch and knocked on the door.

From inside the house, LaMonica and Bishop could see that it was Mama at the door. LaMonica ran to answer it.

"So, you moved around here, now that you're 17, huh?"

"Yeah, Mama."

"Do you still want to go shopping for your birthday gift?"

Before LaMonica could get the words out, Bishop came running up from the back.

"Mrs. Powers, I'm gonna need you to get 300 feet away from my house!" Bishop said it loud and like he meant it.

"This is my daughter; you can't keep me from seein' my daughter!" Mrs. Powers retorted.

"Ain't nobody tryin' to keep you from yo' daughter, but you gonna get away from my house. 300 feet away, to be exact!"

LaMonica just stood there stunned. Never had Bishop told her this was his plan for Mama. She wasn't really mad at him for doing it; after the way Mama had treated him, she was just taken by surprise. That was her first clue that Bishop was a man of revenge. The clue most likely flew over her head, though, but there would be others to come.

Bishop came outside on the porch to emphasize his point. He began pointing out directions to Mrs. Powers.

"You see all of this over here? This is my property, and you can't be on it. I need you to move off my porch and off my property, and out of my driveway. You need to be 300 feet away from my house. Nah, how you like that?"

"I don't have to come to your house," Mama said with an attitude.

"But that's my daughter, and you can't keep me from seein' my daughter."

"Like I said, LaMonica can see you any time she wants to. But it ain't gonna be on my property."

Mama promptly went and moved her car across the street. LaMonica went across the street to talk to her mother through the car window.

"Do you and the baby still want to come with me to the mall to pick out your present?"

"Yeah, okay, Mama."

"Well, go get the baby and the stroller, and let's go."

LaMonica went into the house and grabbed baby Monica. Bishop kissed her goodbye like nothing had happened.

When they arrived at the mall, Mama bought LaMonica the $100 knee-high leather boots she had been eyeing since Christmas. The leather store offered a sale when purchasing two items, so Mama added in a leather purse for LaMonica. And, of course, she picked up a new frilly dress for baby Monica with lacy socks and a headband to match.

Bishop was home waiting on LaMonica to get back from the mall. It was already dark out, and she would need help with the baby. He kept checking the windows for when they would return.

Mrs. Powers pulled up across the street from Bishop's house. He went on the edge of the lawn to wait for LaMonica to cross the street so he could grab the stroller and car seat and help her in the house with the baby. He and Mrs. Powers eyed each other.

"That nigga ain't gonna do nothin' but use you, LaMonica. You'll see."

Mrs. Powers rolled her eyes at Bishop one more time as she drove away.

LaMonica went out shopping again with Mama and Monica soon after that. They didn't come back until the evening time. When she got home, to her surprise Alonzo and Becky (with their baby) were there having a drinking party with Bishop and Gary.

LaMonica didn't know what to think of it. She knew how much Bishop disliked Gary for what he had done to him. He felt somehow slighted at the fact he had to pull back on doing anything about it because his mother asked him to at the time.

Everyone was laughing and playing drinking games and reminiscing about old times from when they were younger. *This can't be right?* LaMonica thought. *Bishop chillin' with Gary, this is the twilight zone.*

LaMonica's bewilderment was all over her face. Bishop spotted it and pulled her aside into their bedroom.

"What is Gary doing here, B? Didn't he try to kill you both? I thought you were still upset about that."

"Baby *I am*."

"Well, it sure doesn't seem like that."

"Baby, do you see all them drinks out there?"

"Yeah," LaMonica responded.

"That square ass nigga bought all that. He just got his check and stopped by buying dranks for everybody. Now I'm gonna get this nigga to run up his tab buyin' me and Lonzo dranks. You want anything?"

"No, B, I'm good. I mean, why would you want to be around somebody that you don't even like? I don't think it's right to use people Bishop."

"Use people? Any other nigga on the street would do way more than I'm doin' right now. At least I ain't whoppin' this nigga's ass. Baby, I can't just let this nigga get away with what he did to me. Now I let him slide back when I was in the hospital, and my mama asked me not to press charges, but he's got to pay one way or another. And today that lil' square ass nigga got to pay."

'Look, you want me to hurt this nigga, or you want me to get some money out of 'em? Cuz one or the two is happening today?"

LaMonica still didn't look satisfied.

"Look, baby, after this nigga buys us some dranks, we'll be square. I won't hold nothin' else against him or try to get back at him. I promise I'll be done with it."

"Okay," LaMonica said with reluctance.

"Now come on out here with us. Lonzo brought Becky by to visit with you."

LaMonica and Becky sat in the dining room, each sipping on a beer while Alonzo, Bishop, and Gary were in the living room.

Becky and LaMonica were playing Uno with regular playing cards. It was something LaMonica often did when she and Bishop visited Aunt Frieda. She wasn't really versed in any other card game except Spades, which most people played in the hood. But Alonzo and some of Bishop's friends could get very serious about it when playing, so LaMonica preferred to stick with simpler games when she could.

The dining room was closest to the kitchen, so Bishop hollered in there for LaMonica to bring him a beer.

"Hey baby, can you bring me another cold beer."

"Okay."

When LaMonica came into the living room, Gary made a remark.

"Man, yo' girl is fine from far away." LaMonica had an acne break out, and that's what he was referring to.

Bishop clenched his jaws, and LaMonica returned to the dining room with Becky.

Alonzo asked Gary about more drinks.

"Hey man, let's run to the store and grab some mo' dranks."

"Alright, sure," Gary responded.

"I've got an idea. Hey, why don't we grab some dranks and all go over to Savannah's house?" Bishop suggested.

"Yeah, that'll be nice," Alonzo said. "Then we can all play some Bones."

Bones was when everybody played Dominoes. That

game was usually pretty relaxed, so LaMonica was cool with it.

"Okay, bet that. Let me grab my dominoes right quick." Bishop said.

LaMonica and Bishop rode in the car with Alonzo and Becky. They dropped Monica off to Mrs. Powers.

"Oh, so I guess that nigga don't have to be 300 feet away when he's in front of my house, huh?"

"Mama, you don't want me to have to walk from across the street with the baby, do you?"

"No, I guess not," Mama said.

Alonzo followed Gary to the liquor store. He and Bishop went inside and picked out whatever they wanted to drink.

Bishop came back out to the car. "Baby, what you and Becky want to drink. This nigga's payin' you might as well grab it."

"I don't know, Bishop. It doesn't matter," LaMonica responded.

"Well, since he's paying, see if you can grab me a case of Miller Lite while you're in their B," Becky said.

Bishop and Alonzo came out with loads of beer. They had cases and 40 ounces of their favorite brands.

They made it to Savannah's house, and she was pleasantly surprised to have Bishop and Alonzo show up at her door on a Friday night with cases of drinks.

"Come right on in y'all. Come right on in."

"Awe, there's my little cousin. She started playing with Becky and Alonzo's baby. Where's little Monica?"

"She's at my mom's," LaMonica said.

Savannah's 10-year-old daughter, Caira, was there. She sent her in the room to watch movies while the adults were in the living room.

Bishop and Alonzo were encouraging Gary to drink faster.

"Hey man, you better hurry up and catch up. Turn yo' drank up," Alonzo said.

Soon Gary was pretty well plastered. Bishop and Alonzo had drunk a lot but were able to hold their alcohol.

Out of nowhere, Bishop and Alonzo changed up.

"Hey nigga, what's that mess you said about my girl earlier?" boom, wham, punch. Bishop punched Gary directly in his face. Gary stood up from the chair.

"Nawl, sit down nigga. Remember when you almost killed my brotha?" wham, punch. Alonzo hit Gary a second time.

Gary was in no shape to fight back. He was crying, "Stop, please stop."

LaMonica was astonished that out of nowhere, Bishop had done this. She soon realized, he and his brother must have had this planned the whole time. They were just looking for any reason to get it started.

Becky jumped up and got in the middle of Gary and Bishop, and Alonzo while holding her baby. This caused them to back off because they didn't want the baby to get hurt. Gary took it as his opportunity to run. He ran straight into Caira's room and locked himself in there with her.

Savannah was begging him to open the door. "Please come out of there with my daughter, Gary."

Caira was crying, but she couldn't get out because Gary was inside blocking the door. He had a serious mental disorder. He didn't know how to fight, and to top it off, he was highly intoxicated.

Savannah was terrified that in Gary's state, he would hurt Caira.

"Somebody call the police. Somebody call the police," Gary was screaming.

Bishop and Alonzo were urging Gary to open the door and let the little girl out. Everyone could hear her crying for her mother.

"Let my baby out of there, Gary!" Savannah commanded.

"Not until they leave," Gary said.

"Bishop, let's just go. You see he's in there crying, and the little girl's in there crying. Let's go," LaMonica said.

"No, I'm not leavin' until I know my little cousin is gonna be okay. I'll punish that nigga if he does anything to her."

"I don't think he'll hurt her," Savannah said. "If y'all go ahead and leave, he'll probably just come on out."

"You sure, cuz, because I'll kick the door down," Alonzo said.

"No! No! Don't kick the door down, then I'll get in trouble with my landlord."

Bishop and Alonzo refused to leave without knowing Gary would come out of Savannah's house, and Caira was okay.

"Look, man, we square now. Ain't nobody gonna hurt you. Just come on out of there so we can make sure Caira is okay. Look, man, me and Lonzo will stand out here on the porch," Bishop yelled from the front of the house.

Gary cracked the door of Caira's bedroom open. "Tell them to leave."

"Okay, they're leaving. They just want to make sure Caira is okay," Savannah said.

"Y'all go outside to the car," Gary said through snot and tears.

Bishop and Alonzo went outside, and Gary came out. Caira ran out of the room after him, and Savannah hugged her. She was fine, just scared after such an awkward encounter.

"Is she okay?" Bishop yelled from outside.

"She's fine, everybody."

"Alright, we gonna take off cuz," Bishop said.

They all got in the car and left. Riding home, LaMonica realized just how serious Bishop was about vendettas between his 300 feet rule with Mama and what he planned out and did to Gary that night.

13

REALITY CHECK

That first day when LaMonica had finally moved in with Bishop, she was full of hope and excitement. Now that she had seen his other side, she hoped that wasn't the real Bishop. B had been such a wonderful father to be, minus the financial aspect. And he was so protective of her and baby Monica, she thought, this had to be the right move. Right?

LaMonica was about to receive a hard dose of reality....

Loving protection quickly translated into a lot of rules at Bishop's house. He was strict on LaMonica like a parent. Although he didn't stop her from leaving - he preferred for her to stay at home and not go anywhere.

He gave her so many rules at the house that she often didn't know which one to follow.

One, she was never to open the door for anyone when he wasn't home.

Two, he didn't want her speaking with his friends when he wasn't around.

Three, when he had company, she was not to get caught even glimpsing at any of his friends that came to the house.

Yet, rule number four was –

"Watch that nigga if I leave the room, so he don't steal nothin'."

She got "in trouble" one day when one of Bishop's friends came over, and Bishop went to the back to retrieve something. While he was in the back, his "friend" stole half a pack of his cigarettes.

"Why weren't you watching him?" B scolded.

"I didn't know he was taking your cigarettes."

LaMonica didn't want to be accused of "looking at him," so she watched TV and kept her head down the whole time he was in the living room. Besides, *why would you let anyone in your house "you have to watch" anyway,* LaMonica thought. She and Mama would never have someone in their home that needed "to be watched."

These rules are a no-win catch twenty-two situation with B, LaMonica thought as she blew her breath.

Moving in with Bishop was supposed to be a part of "the greater later" that Bishop had always promised. All while LaMonica had been pregnant that had been his trusty saying, "it'll get greater later, baby." But when would greater be? How long would later come? Baby Monica needed things NOW, and getting on welfare wasn't as easy as Bishop had thought.

Now that the State of Michigan had ended General Assistance (GA) benefits for people without children, lots of Saginaw County residents were pregnant and trying to get on Aid to Dependent Children (ADC), a welfare benefit for mothers with kids. It seems some had made that their financial plan once GA was cut off.

LaMonica would not be able to get an appointment with a caseworker for at least a month unless she could prove she had emergency needs. Under the Emergency Needs

Program, food stamps and money were expedited within a week (sometimes even a day) if the claimant could prove they were in need. People who were frequently on rotation in the welfare system understood this. LaMonica did not.

Bishop drove LaMonica down to the welfare building. She applied for the Emergency Needs Program and was promptly denied. She would now have to wait a month or more out to get an appointment with a caseworker.

For one thing, Bishop had instructed LaMonica not to go down there with her regular clothes on and to put something on raggedy. There was no way LaMonica was going out of the house looking crazy like Bishop suggested. She went to the welfare meeting wearing her regular clothes. This included her Guess jeans outfit, with her long leather trench coat and leather boots Mama had gotten her for Christmas and her birthday.

"What's wrong with you?" Bishop had asked her.

"When you're trying to get something from somebody, you're supposed to show them how desperate you are and look like it."

"They said I don't qualify for emergency needs, Bishop, because I get that check once a month from Mama's Social Security."

"Well then, you need to go over there to yo' mama's house on the 3rd of the month and get that check," Bishop urged.

"Bishop, I don't want to ask my mama for anything. It'll just prove her right."

"Well, if you would have went in there wearing the kind of clothes I told you to wear, they would have gave you emergency funds, and you wouldn't have to be asking yo' mama for money."

Bishop said this in a grave tone. His demeanor was serious. He began to get this way a lot with LaMonica when it came to money.

"Look, LaMonica. Whenever me or my brother was tryin' to get welfare money or some food stamps, we'd go down there in the roughest clothes we owned—holes in our shirts we didn't care. We'd go down there and let 'em know 'I'm hungry, I'm in need. Do your job and give me my benefits now!' That's the way you're supposed to do it. It's not a popularity contest. It's about getting the money you need, LaMonica. You can get a bunch of compliments on your outfit from ya friends you run into at the welfare building, or you can get the help you need. You decide. Which one makes the most sense?"

LaMonica rolled her eyes at Bishop.

"You know what, you ain't a real woman. A real woman knows how to take care of bitness. You just a lil' teeny bopper. That's all you are."

There was no way in the world LaMonica was going around in public looking trashy no matter what Bishop said. There were people there from her school applying for assistance just like she thought there would be. She wasn't putting on a show and looking crazy just so she could get a welfare check faster because Bishop said so.

But she *would* go and try to get her $75 Social Security check from Mama's house. LaMonica already knew how Mama was. She would not want her to have that Social Security check as long as she lived at Bishop's house. But the lady at the window in the welfare office instructed her to write down all of her income. LaMonica told her about the check and that she didn't know if she would have access to it now that she moved out of Mama's house.

"Honey, that money is solely for your benefit. Your mother wouldn't even receive that extra check if you weren't her dependent. That money is for you and your use and rightfully yours."

What the lady at the welfare office said might have been correct, but Mama worked for that money, and even though that check was in her name, if Mama didn't want her to have it, maybe she should just leave it alone. LaMonica hemmed and hawed over this as it got closer to the 3rd day of the month when Social Security checks are released.

In the meantime, Monica was getting low on diapers. Bishop and LaMonica went to the pawnshop and pawned their "wedding bands." They had the idea that they would one day come back and retrieve them, but they never did. The pawnshop didn't offer them much money for the rings. Bishop kept the money from his wedding band to buy drinks and cigarettes.

LaMonica was working with a little over $20 to buy diapers. That wasn't going to last the entire month. So, on the morning of the 3rd when Bishop woke up early and said, "Hey baby, let's go around the corner and get yo' check." LaMonica agreed.

Thankfully the 3rd rolled around on a Monday that month and Mama had a client she went to see on Mondays, so she wasn't home. LaMonica ran to the mailbox and grabbed the Social Security check addressed to her.

As soon as LaMonica cashed the check Bishop was trying to get money from her for beer and cigarettes.

"I'm using this money for the things that Monica needs, Bishop."

"But what about the water bill? Aren't you at least going to pay the water bill at the house?"

"No, I'm going to buy our baby some diapers and the things that she needs. $75 is not enough money to pay a bill and do that."

LaMonica used her mere $75 Social Security dependent check to buy diapers and wipes for the baby. She was starting to grow out of her clothes that LaMonica had bought while she was pregnant, so she had to buy her clothing with that as well.

Luckily, she didn't have to buy formula because a government program called WIC supplied her with formula monthly. LaMonica had tried breastfeeding Monica when she was first born but quickly became embarrassed (as a teenager with her boob out) every time someone came over to see the baby. She had stopped about 2 weeks into it.

LaMonica did a pretty good job with the limited funds she was working with, but the $75 went pretty quick. She mentioned to Bishop that maybe he should get a job, and he had a whole lot of excuses as to why it's hard for a Black man to get a job, especially with a record.

On the one hand, LaMonica could understand where he was coming from, but on the other hand, he didn't even try. What he did do was get up early every morning like he had a job and go around in the neighborhood collecting random things for trade. Once, he came home with a collection of wine glasses and shot glasses somebody had taken from the Sportsman's Bar over on 3rd Street.

"Look here, baby, these is some good glasses. All you got to do is wash them up, and they'll be worth somethin'."

The glasses were dirty from the bar and had dried-up drinks still in the bottom of them. LaMonica couldn't see how these held any value at all. She especially didn't see how this could benefit Monica.

Bishop always had his trusty saying, though, "It'll get greater later, baby."

One day while Bishop was out scavenging around the neighborhood, a letter came for him that LaMonica couldn't resist opening. It had the return label of Saginaw County Prosecutor's Office - Child Support Division.

Child Support Division? CHILD SUPPORT DIVISION? CHILD SUPPORT DIVISION!

What is this? LaMonica thought.

She double-checked it. It was not addressed to Alonzo, no this letter was addressed to Bishop Holmes. *But how? How?* One thing LaMonica prided herself on was the fact that Bishop didn't have multiple kids with multiple women like a lot of the men in the hood did. At least she wasn't a statistic. *And now this!*

She ripped open the letter. She didn't care if Bishop did get mad about her opening his mail; this couldn't wait.

LaMonica scanned over the legal document with fury. A child had been born, and the mother was naming Bishop as the father because she had sought welfare benefits and was required to do so. The child's name was very odd. It was a female child with a boy's name. And the last name didn't match the surname of either Bishop or the mother.

What could this mean? LaMonica thought.

She scanned for the child's birthdate. The child was born almost two years ago. *Well, at least we weren't together*, LaMonica thought. *But why would he keep this from me?*

LaMonica began pacing the floor. She couldn't wait for Bishop to walk through that door.

When he did, she passed the paper to him, "What is this Bishop? Why didn't you tell me about this?"

"LaMonica, Monica is my only child. I am not this child's father.

'Look, I messed around with the girl once. Then I moved out of town down to Arizona like I told you about before."

"You didn't tell me about the girl part, but okay."

"Baby, that was way back then. Anyway, when I made it

back to Saginaw, she came runnin' up to me talkin' about she was pregnant wit' my baby. I calculated, and the months didn't add up. That girl got pregnant while I was out in Arizona."

"Why didn't you say anything about this to me, Bishop?"

"Because it ain't my baby – baby."

Bishop read through the paperwork and saw that he had a date scheduled to go down to the Prosecutor's Office and take a DNA test. If he didn't show up, he would be defaulted as the father.

"I'm goin' down there to take that test. That ain't my baby."

When the day came, Bishop went alone, without LaMonica. She was home anxiously waiting to see what happened. When Bishop returned, he was all smiles.

"Did you take the test?"

"Nope. She ain't even show up because she knows that ain't my baby."

"What did they say you have to do now?"

"Nothin' it's over. The case is dropped," Bishop said.

"Look, baby, you're my woman, and Monica is *my* baby, nobody else."

"Bishop, I want us to be a family. I don't ever want us to be just "baby mama" and "baby daddy" to each other."

"We are a family, baby. We'll never be that to each other."

LaMonica and Bishop embraced. It was one of the few tender moments they had had (without them arguing over basic needs) since they moved in together.

14

THE COMFORTS OF HOME

Bishop went back to his regularly scheduled program of scavenger hunting all day. He kept bringing things home. Most of them were rarely usable, in LaMonica's opinion.

His latest conquests were coming from neighborhood community centers because he was working on putting a new motor in his car and wanted to clear up all his traffic tickets. Bishop was always going to jail for one thing or another before LaMonica moved in with him. Now that they were living together, he had only been to jail once. After getting out he worked out a deal to have his arrest warrants removed through community service.

One afternoon Bishop brought the baby home some baby cereal from a nonprofit agency where he was doing community service to work off some of his tickets.

"Look here, baby, I got Monica some baby cereal."

LaMonica inspected the date. It was long past due.

"Bishop, this cereal isn't any good; it's past the date."

"Oh, baby, the woman at the center said that doesn't

matter. As long as you check it and it doesn't have any spider webs in it or bugs, it's still good."

LaMonica just looked at Bishop. There was no way she was feeding her baby that mess. Unfortunately, even when Bishop was helping, it wasn't really any help.

LaMonica guessed that this was Bishop's way of contributing. *She* was the one that made sure the baby had what she needed, despite not having much for herself. She had purchased Monica baby jars of food ahead of time, even before she was ready to start baby food, just so that she would already be prepared.

Baby Monica had plenty of formula and food, but the same could not be said around the house for LaMonica. There was often no meat to complete meals, just cans of beans or cans of vegetables. LaMonica didn't know how to live like this.

Bishop would be out all day either doing community service, out in the neighborhood getting scraps for money (which he never brought home), or somewhere running around in one of his old vehicles when he could get one running. He usually ate lunches and snacks at the various community centers. LaMonica would take care of Monica all day and hope he was coming home with some meat or something she could use for dinner for herself.

Each and every time, Bishop would come home with some old junk (probably stuff he scrapped upon and couldn't sell).

"What am I going to do with this Bishop? I thought you were coming home with some meat, or food, or something to eat."

"Baby, you could have been ate. Look at all these cans of vegetables from the soup kitchen around here."

"Okay, Bishop, but there's no can opener or anything to go with the can goods."

"Look, girl, all you have to do is take a butcher knife and cut these cans. If you ain't got no meat, then you improvise and eat the canned vegetables. You actin' like a lil' teeny-bopper LaMonica. You don't know how to survive!"

And that was the problem right there, LaMonica thought. *Why should I have to survive? I didn't come from a house where I was just surviving, so why would I start now?* As hard as it was to admit, LaMonica was beginning to miss the comforts of home.

To top it off, living at Bishop's house was dismal. Oh, it had been fun when she was running away or just sneaking around there for sex but living there was a whole 'nother matter. For one thing, the house was big and empty with barely any furniture. There was an old dusty couch in the living room that smelled like dogs had once used it for their beds. The walls were painted a muted color of depression gray. There was no phone or cable TV, and LaMonica just couldn't relax there.

As a result of this, after spending so much time fighting so hard to have her freedom, she ended up at Mama's house every single day to get her old comforts of home back. Now, every morning when Bishop got up to run around the neighborhood scrapping, she got up early and got Monica ready, so they could head around the corner to the big yellow house on 5th Street.

LaMonica even felt more comfortable taking showers and dressing at Mama's house than at home with Bishop. There was no room in the budget for anything other than soap at home (besides the baby's stuff). The only lotion at Bishop's house was that cheap kind that itched LaMonica's skin. Her hair was beginning to look wild and untamed because, of course, she couldn't afford any hair products.

She began to look forward to going around the corner every day. Mama had good food in the refrigerator she could just grab. When baby Monica took naps, she could kick back and relax on Mama's comfortable sofa and flip through the channels and watch her favorite movies and shows.

Now that Mama was retired and home most of the day, she would sometimes take LaMonica and the baby out for fun things like garage sailing, shopping, or visits with family. Then they would race back home to watch their favorite soap operas.

After laughing and joking and watching soap operas with Mama, it would be time for LaMonica to head back around the corner home to Bishop. That's when Mama would start.

"You know that nigga ain't doing nothing but using you, right? Just using you for sex and whatever welfare check he can get out of you."

Mama had found out about LaMonica going down to the welfare office and applying because her friend from PWP had told her.

"Yeah, Kim told me how you came down there with your name-brand clothes on and leather coat trying to apply for emergency funds."

"LaMonica, you ain't doin' nothin' but letting that negro make a fool of you. He's got you going down there applying for welfare so he can take your check every month. LaMonica, I taught you better than that. You should know better."

"Mama ain't nobody gonna use me for no check. I promise you that."

"Okay, we're gonna see. You just make sure that baby is well taken care of around that corner. I don't know why you and baby Monica don't just come on home and move back in here with me where you belong. You obviously don't like it around there. You're *here* every day."

Mama would really get started with everything she had to say to LaMonica when she wouldn't agree to move back home.

"Well, I'll tell you what, LaMonica, you'd better not come back here on the 3rd messin' with my mailbox and getting that check. As long as you're living around that corner, you ain't got no business with that check. As a matter of fact, I've told Otis (the next-door neighbor) to come and get the check on the 3rd whenever I'm not at home."

Otis was Ms. Eleanor's son and had moved into her house with his family once she had passed. He respected Mrs. Powers, so anything she asked of him he would pretty much do.

Mama became frustrated that LaMonica had been relentless in her stance to be independent living around the corner at Bishop's house. *Well, if she wants independence, I'll show her what it's really like,* she thought. *She ain't gettin' that Social Security check.*

As a matter of fact, Mrs. Powers had become intensively more and more curious about just what the living situation was like where LaMonica had moved to. Obviously, she couldn't go and inspect it for herself because Bishop had banned her from coming within 300 feet of his house. No, she would have to find out another way. Since LaMonica wouldn't budge and come back home, she decided to put in a phone call to the police.

"Hi, I would like to make a report on my daughter not being at home and endangering the welfare of my grand-daughter."

"How old is your daughter, ma'am?"

"She's 17."

"Mrs. Powers, we can't take a runaway report on a 17-year-old."

"Well, she's living with a man, and she and the baby could be in a dangerous situation."

"Okay, Mrs. Powers, we'll send an officer out to talk with you."

A young female officer arrived at the big yellow house on 5th Street that Mrs. Powers was familiar with.

"What seems to be the problem, Mrs. Powers?"

"My daughter is living around that corner there, on Norman Street with a man. And he ain't doin' nothin' but using her. As a matter of fact, ain't no tellin' what's going on in that house because I'm not allowed over there."

"Well, I can go around there and do a welfare check if you'd like. I know it's hard having your daughter living somewhere else when she should be at home."

"Yes, please. Thank you."

"Okay, I'll come back and let you know what my findings are."

After chit-chatting about people on the force they both knew and having a couple of laughs, the officer headed around the corner to Bishop's house.

It was late and dark when LaMonica heard a knock on the door. Bishop was gone. Now that his car was running again, he sometimes hung out late at night with his friends. He'd often come home in the wee hours of the morning, telling LaMonica about bar fights and even knife fights he'd been in while out.

Most of his friends had done short prison terms (one-two years). They were usually caught with small grams of cocaine on them. Bishop would say that they were selling drugs and just lied and told the police and the judge that it was for their own "personal use" to get lighter sentences.

Sometimes Bishop left the house and stayed out all night with these guys, doing who knows what.

"Who is it?" LaMonica asked.

"Open up. It's the police."

LaMonica opened the door, and the police officer stated she needed to do a welfare check.

"Your mother is concerned about you and the baby, and we need to make sure the child has everything she needs," the officer stated.

"Can I come in?" The officer asked the question, "can I come in?" but her tone said, "you'd better let me in."

She was very forceful, so LaMonica let her in. Besides, she wanted to assure the officer that the baby was fine, so she complied.

"Show me where you keep the baby's food."

LaMonica took the officer to the kitchen and showed her all of Monica's packs of formula. She had enough to last an entire month. She then opened up the kitchen cabinets. Monica had a cabinet that was dedicated to just her baby food. It had jars of food and baby cereal, everything the baby would need.

She then showed her the baby's bottles and the plastic liners that she used inside the bottles. Buying liners could get expensive, but LaMonica had chosen this style of feeding because you could push all the bubbles and air out, and the baby had less chance of suffering from painful gas.

The police officer also directed LaMonica to open up the refrigerator. There wasn't much in there other than Monica's pre-made formula and a couple of dishes Bishop's mother Anna had made them.

"Looks like you need to go grocery shopping."

"The baby has everything SHE needs," LaMonica emphasized. She wanted to keep her focus on the baby.

"I need to see where the baby sleeps." The officer's tone was relatively short. It was almost as if she was disappointed to find there wasn't a problem that she could do something about.

LaMonica led the officer into the bedroom and showed her Monica's bassinette with its lacey frills. She also showed her the drawers with Monica's beautiful clothes inside.

Monica was a happy baby. She was awake, and her cuteness softened the officer's attitude.

"Awe, she's such a beautiful baby."

Monica kicked and smiled.

"Well, I'll let your mom know you're doing okay, but go grocery shopping and get some furniture up in here!" And with that, the officer left.

This was precisely the type of scenario that Anna thought would happen when LaMonica moved out of her mother's house. This is why she had left her job in Detroit to be ready at the call. The problem was LaMonica didn't have a phone, and Anna lived on the other side of town. She would most likely have not made it before the officer left. Although everything worked out, it was a bit degrading for LaMonica.

When Bishop made it home, she told him what had happened.

"Why would you let a police officer in without a warrant?"

"Because I wanted to make sure they knew that Monica was okay."

"Man, I guess," Bishop said.

"But yo' mama is somethin' else."

∼

*T*he weather began to break, and LaMonica's friend Jaqueline moved into the neighborhood. They started spending a lot of time together. Jaqueline had a baby too now. LaMonica now began leaving the house to get fresh air. She and Jacqueline would push their babies in strollers around the neighborhood.

This bothered Bishop to no end. He began to constantly warn LaMonica, "you'd betta not be talkin' to anybody. Oh, it's gonna get back to me if you do."

LaMonica wasn't thinking about other guys anyway, but she made sure to do what he said. Sure enough, Bishop's fears that guys would try to holler at her once she was out walking came true. Two high yellow girls with long hair, walking down the sidewalk pushing strollers, was an automatic attention grabber in the hood.

Guys were constantly rolling up on them (usually there were two in the car), "Hey, what's your name?"

Jacqueline would always give them her name and even tell some of them where she lived. LaMonica pulled out her old snotty attitude from high school, risking being called the B-word (which she often was). Anything was better than getting in trouble with Bishop. She didn't want even a hint that she was speaking to a man to get back to him, so she refused to even be cordial with the guys who pulled up on the side of her and Jaqueline.

"Hey, pretty girl, what's your name?" one guy asked.

"She ain't gonna tell you," Jacqueline would respond for her. Jacqueline already knew from experience that LaMonica wasn't going to talk to any of these guys.

Bishop felt threatened by LaMonica's new walking activities. He was always warning her not to get in trouble by letting guys talk to her and that he was very popular and would find out. "I'll give you enough rope to hang your own self," he would often say.

LaMonica knew it was true too. Even if it just *seemed* like she was doing something wrong, it would get back to Bishop because he and his brother were so popular with "their type of people." And there were a lot of Bishop's "type of people" around the hood.

LaMonica had already gotten in trouble the one time she had gone out clubbing with Alonzo's wife, Becky. It was the first time she had ever been to a club. She was only 17 and surprised they let her in.

It was one of those "bring your own drink" clubs, and so Becky, LaMonica, and Becky's friends were drinking, dancing, and partying to the music. LaMonica wasn't paying any attention, but Becky didn't participate in any of the "sexy dances," but LaMonica did. It was her first time at a club, and she was gonna make the most of it.

The next day as LaMonica and Bishop were riding down the street, people were blowing the horn at him and stopping him to let him know they had seen her at the club last night. He already knew she was going anyway but they mentioned her dancing.

They would drive around another corner, and more guys would pull up behind him.

"Hey, man, pull over. I've got somethin' to talk to you about."

Bishop got back in the car. He was disappointed in LaMonica. "LaMonica, I've got niggas flaggin' me down left and right, telling me you were at the club last night dancing like you didn't have no man."

"I was just dancing, Bishop. I only danced with girls. I didn't dance with any guys."

"Yeah, well Lonzo ain't got niggas flaggin' him down about Becky. She knew how to handle herself. See there you go hanging your own self with that rope."

LaMonica hated having Bishop that disappointed in her but what scared her the most was the fact that he wasn't bluffing. Anything she did (even if it just *appeared to be wrong*) would get back to him, and she would be in trouble. He had always said so. Now she could see he wasn't lying. That's why she was extra snotty to any male who made the mistake of trying to speak to her.

15

CHECK-INS

A fter Mama pulled that stunt, LaMonica decided not to go around to her house every day like she had been doing. She decided to take a break from Mama. This prompted Mrs. Powers to call the police again.

"Can somebody please go check on my daughter? She's living in the house with a man around the corner from me and ain't no tellin' what's happening with that baby."

The police station would send officers out to Mrs. Powers' house but would not continue to do welfare checks on LaMonica and baby Monica.

"Mrs. Powers, we've done a welfare check on your daughter and the baby. They are both fine. The baby has everything she needs."

"Well, the last officer told me they didn't barely have any furniture in that house."

"Mrs. Powers, a lack of décor is hardly a crime."

More and more of the officers who knew Mrs. Powers up close and personal had retired, and they usually sent these new cops out now, who she wasn't familiar with. The inability to get them to work on her team was really frustrating her.

"Mrs. Powers, as police officers, we inspect crimes. No crime has been committed."

Mrs. Powers was well connected with her local community agencies. She often attended community meetings. At one of those meetings, she found out that the Child Protection Services had to respond to any call they received, even calls the police refused to go on. The woman giving the presentation had said even if someone called ninety-nine times and a worker had gone out to find no wrongdoing, if a call came out on the hundredth time, they were still required to go out and inspect. Mrs. Powers decided if LaMonica didn't start coming back to visit, that would be her next call.

In the meantime, LaMonica was home with Bishop reevaluating her life. Some of the things that Mama had said rolled around in her head.

"That nigga ain't doing nothin' but usin' you."

"You ain't got no business living in a house with a man."

Along with Mama's voice in her head, LaMonica felt a spiritual conviction. Like she was so far away from God now that she was living in sin. *Not only am I disappointing Mama, but I'm disappointing God*, she thought.

It was right around this time that two of her friends from church decided to pay her a visit one Sunday morning.

Mrs. Powers had worked a security job guarding the parking lot of another church on Sundays for a while now and hadn't been to Mt. Olive Church in some time. She had recently decided to attend a Wednesday night service. While attending, two of LaMonica's friends from church, Saffron and Brandy, had approached her.

"Hi Mrs. Powers, are LaMonica and the baby here?" Saffron asked.

"Chile, no, she's at her house with the baby."

"Oh, she doesn't live with you anymore?" Brandy asked.

"No, honey, she moved in with her boyfriend."

"Awe, we wanna see the baby."

"Well, if y'all want to see LaMonica, you can go visit her. The house is right down the street here from church. I'll point it out to you. I'm not allowed around there myself."

Saffron and Brandy decided they would visit the following Sunday during the daytime.

Saffron and Brandy had both grown up with LaMonica all their lives. They had all been members of Mt. Olive Baptist Church since they were toddlers. It had been different not having LaMonica in Sunday School class over the last year.

LaMonica dropped out of Sunday School and church when she became pregnant with baby Monica. There was a lot of talk amongst the Black community about girls who fell down and "broke their leg" (which was the saying for an unmarried pregnancy).

Teens getting pregnant in Mama's circle was really frowned upon, especially at Mt. Olive Church. Most of the members came from well-to-do families whose parents either had high levels of education or worked in the GM plant. No, there would be no getting pregnant as a teen at Mt. Olive. All of their bright young people were preparing to head off to college one day. If one of them did have an oopsie, no one knew about it.

LaMonica already knew the looks and the scolding she would get if she showed up to the church pregnant, so she just decided not to attend until she had the baby. In her teenage mindset, being pregnant was the problem; once she showed up with the baby, she thought it would be fine.

Once the baby was old enough to leave the house, LaMonica got her dressed and ready for church. She dressed baby Monica up in one of her pretty frilly pink dresses, added a bow to her hair, and put her on matching lace socks. Monica had on her cute white shoes with bells also.

It was Winter out. LaMonica wrapped Monica in her pink snowsuit and headed for church. She had actually missed attending church and was looking forward to showing everyone the new baby. And now it was "safe" because she wasn't pregnant anymore.

As soon as LaMonica entered the doors of Mt. Olive Church, she was greeted by an usher who had known her all her life. The usher began shaking her head in disapproval immediately.

"Uh – uh - uh! You're just a baby yourself; what you doin' with a baby?"

LaMonica was immediately disheartened. *This* was the greeting she was to receive after being gone for nearly a year?

The headshakes didn't stop there; nearly every adult at church greeted her this way. LaMonica grabbed baby Monica and headed out of there and hadn't darkened the doors of Mt. Olive Church ever since. Obviously, having a baby as a teenager was much too sinful.

Now that she lived with Bishop, they didn't go to church. They didn't even listen to gospel music on Sundays like she did at Mama's house. Bishop owned a bible that his mother had given him as a gift with his name inscribed on it, but they never read it.

Bishop's mother Anna went to church very frequently.

Once or twice LaMonica and Bishop had visited her church, but Bishop was under the impression that you had to clean yourself up first to be worthy in the eyes of God. LaMonica sort of felt that way too. She felt incredibly guilty living in sin with a man and having a baby out of wedlock. Despite her guilt, she often had conversations with God, frequently making deals with Him for when she would be a better person and worthy soon.

LaMonica had been feeling guilt and condemnation when Saffron and Brandy stopped by the house on Norman Street one Sunday morning.

"Hey, come on in!" she greeted them with excitement. LaMonica rarely had a chance to talk with anyone her age anymore. She was often stuck in the house taking care of the baby while Bishop ran around. And whenever she and Bishop interacted with other couples, it was either his older brother Alonzo and his wife or one of his friends or cousins and their girlfriends who were all much older than LaMonica.

"Your Mama told us where you lived, so we thought we would stop by to see how you were doing," Saffron said.

The girls never sat. The sofa didn't look very inviting. When LaMonica offered for them to sit, they said they had to get back to church soon. The girls had just stopped by during the break period from Sunday School to the start of Sunday service.

"You should come to church sometimes," Saffron said.

Brandy nodded in agreement. "Yes, bring the baby. She's so beautiful. Can I hold her?"

"Sure."

LaMonica passed Monica over to Brandy. She and Saffron took turns holding her and cooing over her.

LaMonica had vowed she wouldn't return to church

after the way she had been treated. But now that Saffron and Brandy were making her feel so welcomed, maybe she would give it another shot.

Bishop had been there during the visit.

"Bishop, do you think we could go visit my church soon?"

"Yeah, baby. If you want to."

Eventually, they went to visit, but Bishop was offended at how many times they passed the offering plate around, and they never returned.

～

On Monday morning Bishop and LaMonica had another unexpected visitor, the Child Protection Services (CPS). LaMonica was thankful that they came when Bishop was still home because this was a scary situation.

"LaMonica Powers, we have a report that there may be a case of child endangerment here."

"Child endangerment? That's ridiculous!" Bishop said.

"We're talkin' about a 4-month-old baby. Nobody would ever hurt my baby!" He continued.

"Well, that may be true, but we received a report in, and we're legally obligated to check."

"Baby, I'm runnin' down to the payphone to call my mama," Bishop said.

Bishop ran down to the payphone to call Anna.

"Ma'am, I already showed an officer all of the baby's stuff and how she's doing not that long ago."

LaMonica didn't have a problem complying with them because she wasn't doing anything to hurt the baby, but this felt wrong. Violating even.

"Listen like I told Mr. Holmes, we're legally obligated to

check anyway. We'll get things going, and then we can be out of your hair."

The Child Protection Services worker wasn't short in tone like the police officer had been.

"Do you need to see her food and formula?" LaMonica asked.

"Yes, we'll need to see that too, but first we'll need to see the baby."

"She's right here." LaMonica had been holding her the whole time.

"No, we'll need you to strip her down and take all her clothes off, including her diaper."

Oh my gosh, these people were checking for bruises. This was crazy! LaMonica wanted to do everything possible to show them right away that her baby was fine.

She laid a lap cloth on the couch, and the CPS worker sat on one end of the sofa and watched LaMonica as she removed all of baby Monica's clothing. The worker then picked the baby up and inspected her face, neck, arms, torso, legs, back, head – every inch of her body.

"She's doing good, and she's a happy baby," the worker said.

LaMonica had never felt so degraded. *Nobody could have made this false claim but Mama.*

"We'll need to see her food now."

LaMonica went through the same ritual as she did with the police officer. She showed the worker the refrigerator with her pre-made formula. She showed her the bottles and liners she used for baby Monica and the many cans of formula she had on hand for feeding times. She then showed her the cabinet dedicated to Monica's food, which included baby cereal and baby jars of food.

LaMonica even offered extra things, "Here's her baby

spoon and her teether I keep in the fridge. I have multiple nipples also. I have the special ones that don't make the baby work too hard to get the formula and cut down on air."

This is the CPS; they have the power to do things, extreme things. How could Mama take it this far?

Bishop came back from the payphone. He hadn't been able to get ahold of his mother because she was out working in the field and not at her office, so he left her a message.

Bishop's mother worked for a legal service that often interacted with Child Protection Services, so he let them know who she was.

"My mom is Anna Holmes."

"Oh yes, I know your mom. She's been working in the legal arena for years. She's well known in our circle to get the job done. Just transferred down from Detroit, right?"

"Yes, ma'am, she did," Bishop replied.

"We knew LaMonica's mother was gonna try and pull somethin' like this. That's why she transferred."

"Even though I'm very fond of your mother and the work that she does, Mr. Holmes, I still have to conduct my visit today impartially. But everything appears to be in order here. I just need to see where the baby sleeps."

"She sleeps here," LaMonica directed.

"Here in this bassinette?" the worker asked in a concerned tone.

"Yes." LaMonica expected the worker to be impressed at how nice it was, but she didn't appear to be.

"Hmm, let me see.... based on Monica's birthdate, she's going to be 5 months soon. Is that correct?"

"Yes, next month."

"Okay, that's a problem."

Bishop and LaMonica were petrified. *What was going to happen with their baby?*

"Babies shouldn't be in a bassinette at 5 months because they can begin to roll out at that age. She'll need a crib. What I'll do is get you a referral for an agency for a free secondhand crib. How does that sound?"

"Oh yes ma'am. That sounds wonderful." Bishop and LaMonica were both relieved.

"Also, I'd like to get nurse home visits scheduled monthly for Monica."

"She has a doctor, but if you want the nurse to come out, that's fine," LaMonica replied.

"Great. I'll have the nurse bring your crib referral when it's ready, and once she has it set up, we can close your case."

"Okay, thank you, ma'am," LaMonica stated as the CPS worker left.

LaMonica could not **BELIEVE** that Mama had done this, but at least baby Monica was getting a crib at the end of it all.

16

THE QUEEN WAS ALWAYS A PAWN

Bishop and LaMonica received a letter from the welfare department. The day was finally scheduled for them to meet with a caseworker to receive an Aid to Dependent Children (ADC) welfare check. The closer it got to the time of their scheduled interview, the antsier Bishop got.

"Look here, baby, you know you're supposed to give me half that check, right?"

LaMonica looked at Bishop with confusion and annoyance.

"LaMonica, that check is to help pay bills at this house. And since I pay the bills, you're supposed to give me at least half of that check."

"No Bishop, because you own this house outright. There's no rent to be paid on this house, so I don't need to give you any money to cover rent."

"What about the power bill for lights and gas, LaMonica? What about the water bill and the taxes on the house?"

LaMonica rolled her eyes at Bishop and flipped her lip up Elvis Presley style. She would not be like the other women in the neighborhood on welfare and giving a man their check. She was NOT going to be what Mama said she would turn out to be.

She didn't care what Bishop was saying. All it sounded like to her was him trying to get his hands on some money. And she was using that check for her baby and their needs only. How had Bishop been paying the water bill and the power bill before she moved in?

"Look Bishop, Monica needs a lot of things. She needs diapers constantly. She needs baby powder. She needs baby oil, wipes, hair things. She needs dresses and clothing. I can't split the money with you."

Like Mama had said, LaMonica wasn't raised to be no fool, and the more Bishop pressed her about money, the more she started to feel he was trying to make her into one. And she wasn't falling for it.

On the day of the appointment, she and Bishop went together to meet with the caseworker. The caseworker told LaMonica and Bishop they were finally approved for Aid to Dependent Families and children (AFDC/ADC), and they would begin receiving a welfare check with both of their names on it to the home twice a month.

In Bishop's excitement, he urged the caseworker, "Can you please explain the rules to her, ma'am? The check is in both of our names, so we're supposed to cash it, and she's supposed to give me half, right?"

"The check is for your household bills and the care of your child. If there's anything left after that (which shouldn't be much), then yes, you would split it in half." The caseworker didn't know if these young people understood that with $385 a month, if there was anything left to split after bills, it probably wasn't much over $10.

As they were leaving in the car, Bishop began reiterating

to LaMonica what her responsibilities were when it came to the welfare check.

"You heard the caseworker, right? You're supposed to give me half of the check every month."

"No, that's not what she said, Bishop. She said we split anything that's left over after the bills are paid."

LaMonica could see this check situation was going to be a problem with Bishop. But she was determined not to give in. She was determined not to get used like Mama said she would. In the end, she did give Bishop half of the remaining check, and she lost more and more respect for him because of it.

Bishop's brother Alonzo was proud of him for getting a woman to give him some money. In his eyes, that's what you're supposed to do. Operate like a pimp towards women. Most of Bishop's friends were this same way. He often felt "lacking" because he hadn't been able to pull it off up until this point, like his peers.

When the first check arrived, it was a little short of the amount the caseworker said she would be getting. The ADFC caseworker made a visit to inspect the house—which was part of the requirements for receiving assistance. During the visit, she told LaMonica that her check amount would be short because they were deducting her monthly dependent Social Security income from it.

"But I don't have access to that check," LaMonica explained.

"My mom won't let me have it every month."

"Well, it's registered as part of your income just the same, and so we have to deduct it."

LaMonica made a long list of everything that baby Monica needed ,and she ordered some furniture for Bishop's dismal house. She would tie up most of the money before she gave Bishop half of a check.

Bishop didn't care. He still emphasized he needed half of whatever was left over, and so LaMonica gave in and lost more and more respect for him. It got to the point that she didn't even want him to touch her. She was less and less attracted to him physically.

She felt tricked, bamboozled. This had all been *his* plan. Have a baby, move in with him and get on welfare. LaMonica was beginning to believe that greater would never come; especially after the time he gave her that pimp slap (while discussing Lucas and Renee).

If only she would have come into the realization that Bishop had conned her into having a baby for his own personal gain; she could've saved herself from so many hardships. He was just as horrible as his brother Alonzo. He just didn't have the looks to pull off being a womanizer like him.

Despite LaMonica's harsh treatment from Ms. Demona growing up, she had still been spoiled and privileged when it came to Mama. She lived in the hood, but she was raised as an only child and not hoodlike. Mama worked jobs that only paid a couple of dollars over minimum wage, but she owned her own home and, of course, later had a Social Security check. LaMonica was used to getting her own way and having nice things. When she was a child, if Mama couldn't afford them, then her brother Richard would make sure she received them.

LaMonica was used to being treated like a queen, or at the very least, a princess. There's nothing more eye-opening than a queen realizing she's been played like a pawn. And that was EXACTLY what Bishop had been doing. As time went on, she would see more examples of this.

Once when they were over to Anna's house for dinner, Bishop's father, Alonzo Sr., was there. He had started working as a handyman and had a big job for Bishop to help him with. It wasn't much money, but Bishop hadn't held over a hundred dollars in his hands in a while. After dinner, he and his father were going to head off to the job while LaMonica and baby Monica visited with Anna.

Anna wanted to take Monica by her sister's house and show her off. When she went to put her shoes on, they were too tight.

"LaMonica and B, Monica's shoes are too tight," Anna yelled. "She needs some new ones right away."

"Okay, Ma. Her mama's gonna be gettin' her some soon. Right, baby?"

"Yeah, I didn't realize they were too small. She keeps her socks on around the house most of the time."

"Well, when will you be gettin' her some?" Anna asked.

"Probably in a couple of weeks when I get my check," LaMonica responded.

"Oh nonsense. This baby needs the right shoes on her feet now! Come on, we're gonna run to the store and grab her a new pair."

"All right," LaMonica said with excitement.

"You and the baby go get in the car. Let me holler at B's dad really quick."

LaMonica and Anna drove out to the mall and bought baby Monica a pair of name-brand shoes in her correct size. Then they went and visited with some of Anna's family with the baby. When they returned to the house, Bishop pulled LaMonica aside.

"Why did you agree to let my mama buy those shoes? Now my daddy says how much ever they cost he's takin' that out of my cash for the handy work job. How much was it anyway?"

"It was just $40, Bishop."

"That's $40 out of my money."

LaMonica was floored. How was Bishop acting like this over having to buy his own daughter some shoes? He had never bought her anything of significance since her birth, really. The only thing Bishop had outright bought Monica up until that point was that pack of socks from back when LaMonica was pregnant.

As Monica grew, her needs became more and more expensive. LaMonica got help where she could. For instance, there was an organization called Abortion Alternatives. They gave out clothing once a month to mothers and supplied baby formula to help with the overlapping days between when the WIC coupons ran out and it was time to get more. They also gave out a handful of diapers to needy families once a month.

The Abortion Alternatives resource was a great one. Still, they had limited funding as they were trying to help a great number of people. As Monica aged as a baby and her needs became more expensive, sometimes these resources didn't quite cover the gap.

Now that she was a mother, LaMonica better understood how much things costs for a child and that a monthly welfare check of $385 was nowhere near enough money to take care of a baby. She urged Bishop to get a job.

This ticked him off. *What is this change up LaMonica is tryin' to bring? This wasn't in the plan.* His plan was for her to get a welfare check and get more money comin' in, not for him to have a job.

As things began to get tight financially, LaMonica bit her pride and headed back around the corner to 5th Street, where Mama was. Of course, there she heard almost daily from Mrs. Powers that she was being used living around that corner on Norman Street with Bishop. Daddy still wasn't talking to her, and Birdie and her brothers were out of town. Mama was her only support system. She always had been honestly.

LaMonica felt like a fool having to ask Mama for the things she needed against her own pride. Whenever she would bring this up to Bishop, he would just say, "Listen, baby, I know things are hard now because I don't have the money that you want me to have for our child but trust me, it gets greater later."

Bishop had a ton of rhyming sayings that produced a lot of feel-good feelings but not much action. LaMonica had held out hope for too long that what B was saying was true - "It'll get greater later."

She was disappointed in him. Now that she had had the baby, Bishop didn't do anything to support her. He didn't help her with anything financially for baby Monica.

Even though LaMonica didn't agree with Mama to her face when she complained about Bishop, she processed everything Mama would say. As time went on, B's actions or lack thereof did not escape her.

Things came to a head one day when LaMonica calculated all the money she had to spend on Monica's needs and pay the furniture bill. Bishop refused to not only get a job, but he continued to want half of any left over money LaMonica had from that welfare check. She had begun dwindling the amount of money she would give Bishop down to $40 a month.

"Bishop, you need to get a job. The baby is running out of her diapers and formula before the end of the month every month, and I keep running around to free places trying to cover it, but it's getting tight. Why can't you get a job?"

The tone was getting serious in the room.

"I ain't neva'... eva'... punchin' no honkey's clock," Bishop declared.

"Why? Why not Bishop? You ain't doin' nothin' else all day."

"LaMonica, I'm out here hustlin' every day."

Hustlin', that was a joke. The most hustlin' LaMonica had ever seen Bishop do was that time he and Alonzo went to Montana to rob illegal farmers of their Marijuana fields. Alonzo connected with an ex-inmate he had been locked up with who had moved out there. He said that the farmer's Marijuana fields were open and easy to get to.

One weekend Bishop and Alonzo took a trip to Montana and stole Marijuana by the pounds. They had garbage bags upon garbage bags of full, grown, Marijuana plants in the trunk. They brought it back to the house and hung it from the ceiling in a room in the back of the house.

LaMonica hadn't ever seen Bishop so excited about how much money he was going to make. She went to the back of the house to look at the plants at his urging. There was Marijuana for days hanging in that room.

"Baby, all it's got to do is dry out. Then it'll be ready to sell."

LaMonica just watched Bishop.

The plant wasn't drying out fast enough for him, so he placed some plants in the oven. He and some of his friends tried to smoke it. It did not get them high. Then he poured gin on another batch and placed it in the oven. The only thing it did for him and his testers was caused them to cough and choke. No one would be getting high off of this weed, and it was no more fit to sell for drugs than the plants in Mama's yard. Bishop even sucked at being a criminal. *He might as well get a job,* LaMonica thought.

He always claimed he was hustlin', but he NEVER brought any money home. It just didn't add up. Back when LaMonica was visiting at Mama's house, she would talk to her friends on the phone. They were all telling her there was a rumor out that Bishop was on drugs. That he and his brother Alonzo were both crack heads.

"Hustlin'? Bishop, please. You're gone day and even night when your car is running so called hustlin'; yet you never buy Monica anything. I'm to the point where I can't stand you anymore. I'm ready to move back around the corner to my mama's house."

"Oh, you can't stand me? Is that right? Okay, Okay!

'Well dig this here, LaMonica, I'm gonna make you hate me then. Go on back around to ya mama's house. You ain't a real woman anyway. You can't even half cook. You ain't nothin' but a lil' teeny bopper. A real woman knows how to please her man and take care of him, like Renee and Becky.

'Oh, and just to let you know, you ain't takin' that furniture out of this house either. It's staying right here wit' me."

In anger, LaMonica grabbed one of the nicest things Bishop owned in that house: his glass end table and threw it at him, shattering it all over the floor.

"You know what, LaMonica, hurry up and get yo' stuff and get out of here. The baby, she doesn't have to go anywhere, but you—you have to get out of here."

LaMonica went and got baby Monica and put her in her stroller, along with what clothes she could fit in it, and headed around the corner for Mama's.

"I'm coming back to pick up the rest of my stuff."

"Nawl take it all with you now, cuz you ain't coming back ova here."

"I can't carry all that stuff with the baby, Bishop."

"Well, you should have thought about that before you broke my glass table. B%*% run on."

LaMonica walked into Mama's house carrying some of Monica's clothes and what little things she could haul from Bishop's house.

"Mama, I'm done with Bishop. This nigga is talking about he ain't never gonna get a job. Then he disrespected me."

"He didn't put his hands on you, did he?"

"No, Mama, he didn't do that." Bishop hadn't hit her today, but LaMonica would never tell Mama about the time Bishop had slapped her when they were riding in the car. She might kill him, and Monica would end up without a father.

"Okay, well, let's run around there and get yo' stuff."

"He said I can't have my stuff, Mama, only what I could carry when I first left. And he won't let me get my furniture either."

"Oh, we'll see about that. Come on, let's head around this corner. That nigga's gonna give you yo' stuff or he'll have to deal with me!"

LaMonica jumped in the car with Mama and headed back around the corner to Bishop's house. Mama pulled in front of Bishop's house instead of across the street like usual. She would have pulled into the driveway, but Alonzo's car was there. 300 feet didn't mean anything to her that day.

Bishop had been inside the house constantly looking out of the windows for when LaMonica would return. He had a strong suspicion she was coming back with Mrs. Powers. Alonzo happened to stop over, and when Bishop told him everything that had happened, he was fighting mad. If it wouldn't tick Bishop off, Alonzo would love to grab LaMonica by the collar and show her, her place.

As soon as Mrs. Powers' car pulled up on the side of the street closest to his house, Bishop knew what time it was. He ran out onto the porch.

"Nawl Mrs. Powers, get away from my property. You ain't supposed to be within 300 feet of my house, remember?"

"That ain't valid. You ain't got no restraining order. LaMonica is coming in there and getting her stuff, and you better not put yo' hands on her."

"Ain't nobody tryin' to put they hands on yo' daughter Mrs. Powers."

"Then let her come in there and get the rest of her and the baby's stuff."

"Fine, whatever," Bishop answered.

LaMonica jumped out of the car.

"Wait, LaMonica, let me come in there with you."

"No, Mama, I can go alone; can you just stay in the car with the baby?"

"Alright, but I'll be watching."

As soon as LaMonica stepped inside the house, Bishop had all of her stuff in a pile on the living room couch. He wanted to limit her movements in the house.

"All yo' stuff is right there, so you can grab it and take it to the car."

"What about the baby's cans of formula in the kitchen?" LaMonica asked this as she made her way towards the kitchen. When she did that, Alonzo came from upstairs and cut her off from entering the kitchen.

"You ain't going in this kitchen. Like B said, everything you need is on that couch. Yeah, I'd like to see you throw a glass table at me like you did my brother. Run up so you can get done up!"

Bishop didn't want his brother to hurt LaMonica. So, he ran to the kitchen and grabbed the formula and placed it on the sofa.

LaMonica started carrying the cans of formula and all her clothing out to the car. After she had carried out everything that had been laid out on the couch, she walked towards the bedroom.

"Uh uh, what you doing?" Bishop asked.

"Monica still has clothes in here and I need them."

Alonzo started moving towards LaMonica.

"I got this, bro," Bishop jumped in.

"You sure you good, bro?" Alonzo didn't want to leave Bishop in the house with LaMonica in case Mrs. Powers came in there trippin' with a bat, tear gas, a gun, or who knows what.

"Yeah, I'm sure. I'm good. I can handle this. I'll meet up with you at yo' house after all this is over."

"Alright, holla' at me if you need me. I'll come running." Alonzo said this as he looked at LaMonica like she was something he wouldn't mind mopping the floor with. LaMonica was one of those chicks that thought she was all that; he would relish in the opportunity to prove her wrong.

After Alonzo left, LaMonica went into the bedroom, demanding that she get all of her baby's stuff.

"Go head and get it, LaMonica, but I hope this doesn't mean you're gonna try to keep my baby from me."

"Nobody is trying to keep your daughter from you, Bishop, but she needs all of her things.

'And I want all of my furniture too."

"You ain't getting that furniture. It's in this house, and it ain't goin' nowhere."

"I paid for that furniture with my money."

"That check was in both our names, so technically, we both paid for it."

LaMonica grabbed all of her and baby Monica's remaining items from the bedroom. After making several trips back and forth to the car, she was finished except for the crib.

"What about the baby's crib? She needs it, Bishop."

Bishop's attitude had softened towards LaMonica now that he realized she was really gone. "I'll take it apart and bring it around to yo' Mama's house later."

And with that, LaMonica left.

"Did you get everything?" Mrs. Powers asked.

"Everything except for my furniture. He won't let me take that out of the house, Mama."

"That nigga can't keep your furniture. You can take him to court about that."

LaMonica decided she would just worry about that later.

17

RUMORS

W hen LaMonica returned home, her friends and her cousin Olivia began stopping over. Mama had told her some of them had revealed they hadn't visited much with her because they didn't care for Bishop. He was controlling, and they didn't like how he talked to her, but somehow, she didn't seem to notice it.

Lynn had moved from the suburbs to the East Side. Olivia lived in Bridgeport, which technically is a suburb of the East Side. They had both heard more things about Bishop they thought were important to share. Lynn especially had her ear out to the streets and knew about these things.

"A couple of my homeboys said they sold drugs to Bishop?"

"What like weed?" LaMonica asked.

"No, not weed, crack rocks!" Lynn exclaimed.

"Yeah, he is skinny like a crackhead, LaMonica," Olivia added.

"He's always been skinny, though, ever since I've known

him. I just think that's his makeup."

Lynn and Olivia just looked at each other while LaMonica continued on in her defense of Bishop.

"And he was probably just getting some drugs to resell," LaMonica continued.

Bishop often claimed to be doing various hustles, including selling drugs, although LaMonica never saw him with any money.

"LaMonica, my homeboy, said he was just buying one rock at a time. That's not how people buy crack to sell it."

LaMonica had a hard time wrapping her mind around Bishop being a crack addict. Didn't crack addicts steal from everybody, including family? Although she suspected Bishop stole things for money, he had never taken anything from her or his mama and Aunt Frieda.

LaMonica decided she wouldn't put too much stock into rumors. Still, she would ask Bishop about it when she felt like talking to him again.

That opportunity didn't take long; Bishop called her from his mother's house the next day.

"My mama needs to know if we can come and pick up the baby."

"Yeah, that's fine," LaMonica responded.

"You should come too, LaMonica, so you can help with her while she's here," Anna said from the background.

"Here, my mama wants to talk to you." Bishop passed the phone to Anna.

"You might as well get out of the house and come on over here with lil' Monica."

"Well, me and Bishop broke up, Anna, and I'm not really trying to be around your son right now."

"Oh, ain't nobody worried about what you and B got going on, honey. It's a nice day out, we're getting ready to grill, and you need to bring that baby over here. It's a family grill day. Lonzo and Becky will be here with their baby too."

Little did Anna know that saying Alonzo would be there was not exactly a selling point for LaMonica. She was so inviting, however, including her and the baby in a family day, it was hard to turn her down.

LaMonica hesitated.

"Look, if you want, I'll pick you up by myself. That way, you won't have to ride in the car with B."

"Alright, me and the baby will be ready." LaMonica relinquished her stance. A barbeque did sound nice.

Anna picked LaMonica and baby Monica up and brought them to her house. The smell of fresh cut grass was in the air. Anna's home was a beautiful atmosphere to pull up to. Her yard was well kept like Mama's, and she lived in a nice neighborhood. Outside B's dad had stopped by, and he was grilling with Alonzo and Bishop.

As soon as Bishop saw LaMonica get out of the car, he came running up.

"Hey baby." He directed this at LaMonica.

"I'm not your baby," LaMonica responded.

At the same time, baby Monica was jumping up and down with excitement in LaMonica's arms at the sight of her daddy.

"Awe, come here. Daddy misses you too." Bishop grabbed Monica and held her.

It was something to see how excited Monica got about her daddy.

"I miss seeing her every morning, beating me in the head with her rattle."

Bishop and LaMonica both laughed.

Aunt Frieda was inside, and she lit up when she saw Bishop and LaMonica together with the baby.

"Now that's how it's supposed to be, LaMonica and Bishop. You, LaMonica, and baby Monica all together because I know for a fact that y'all truly love one another."

LaMonica and Bishop ended up having a conversation off to themselves while baby Monica was napping.

"I can't believe you threw a glass table at me."

"I can't believe you wouldn't let me have my furniture."

"Well, how else was I gonna have a way to hold on to you? I needed a reason for you to still come back to the house. Even if it was just to argue with me about getting your furniture back."

The next thing everyone knew, LaMonica and Bishop were in an embrace and kissing. Anna, Aunt Frieda, and everyone else knew it wouldn't be too long before Bishop and LaMonica were back together.

When Anna brought LaMonica and baby Monica home, Bishop rode in the car with them. Mama saw how cozy they were when LaMonica got dropped off.

"I hope you don't plan on gettin' back with that nigga," Mama said.

LaMonica didn't respond as she unpacked Monica from her car seat and got her ready to wash up for bed.

"LaMonica, you ain't nothin' but a fool if you get back with that negro. And I don't want him around here at my house."

"But Mama, how is he supposed to come see the baby?"

"That's between y'all, but I don't want him around here at my house, and that's final Ms. Powers." Calling LaMonica Ms. Powers was the clue she always gave that she had the real power and not her.

Welp, LaMonica knew what that meant. And if she didn't want to cause Bishop to get a bat taken to his current ride, she'd better follow Mama's directions.

Bishop had been asking LaMonica to move back in with him. She felt like Mama was pushing her to have no choice but to take him up on his offer. She couldn't just go walking around there to visit Bishop with the baby because often he was out running around. She would have no way of knowing for sure if he was home or not because he didn't have a phone. The thought of dragging Monica around the corner with all her stuff just to turn back around seemed too much of an endeavor.

The next day Bishop called LaMonica from his mother's house.

"Hey baby," Bishop spoke to LaMonica like they were never broken up.

"Heeey," LaMonica replied with excitement.

Mama could tell based on LaMonica's tone alone that it was Bishop on the other line, and she had warmed back up to him.

"LaMonica, is that that nigga on the phone?"

LaMonica just looked without answering, which told Mama everything she needed to know.

"Hang up. I don't even want that nigga callin' my house. He ain't doin' nothin' but trying to convince you to come back around that corner."

"I gotta go, Bishop."

"Okay, but listen, I'll be at my Mama's house most of the day. Call me back when your mama leaves."

"Okay."

Mama having this stance put LaMonica right back into the mindset of having to fight for love with Bishop again. As soon as Mama pulled out of the driveway, she called Bishop. The rumors of Bishop being a crack head were heavy on her mind, and with so much family being around, she hadn't had a chance to ask him about it at the barbeque the other day.

"Bishop, my friends are telling me their boyfriends are saying they've sold you drugs to use."

"Your friends who?"

"Bishop. Have you been buying drugs?"

"Baby, you already know anytime I buy drugs, it's to hustle."

LaMonica reflected back to how many times she had heard Bishop saying he was hustlin', but yet he NEVER had any money. She also thought about how all his friends were older and looked like drug users. They would always say that they were lying about having drugs for personal use when the police caught them so they could be sentenced to a drug program and have a lighter sentence. But honestly, they all looked like they were telling the truth when they said, "personal use."

Not that selling drugs was okay either. Whenever Bishop claimed that's what he had been doing, LaMonica would tell him she wasn't okay with that or the type of danger it could bring upon the whole household when they lived together. But as a teenager, it was much more cooler to have a drug dealer for a boyfriend than a crack head.

"It's a whole lot of people that be hatin' and lyin' on me and my brother. My mama asked me the same thang. She said somebody came to her saying I was on drugs. I was like, 'what'?

'She asked me, 'why am I so skinny?' I told her my daddy's slim, of course I'm gonna be slim too. Ain't nobody on drugs.

'I told you before LaMonica I ain't neva' did nothin' but smoked weed and tried snortin' cocaine that one time with my cousin. I ain't like it. That ain't me."

Bishop had told LaMonica this before because back when she was pregnant, she had heard rumors of him being on drugs then too. *The way he looked and dressed, maybe it wasn't just because he was living in a hard situation. Maybe there was something else to it,* she thought at the time.

At first, when LaMonica was pregnant but not showing, Bishop went around telling everyone he knew that he and LaMonica were having a baby together. He even told friends of hers that lived in his mother's neighborhood.

Bishop got around a lot, and he ran into a large number of people constantly. Eventually, friends and people from all over Saginaw were calling to ask LaMonica if she was pregnant by Bishop. At first, out of shame for being a teenager and pregnant and out of embarrassment for how Bishop looked and dressed, coupled with the drug rumors that were going around about him - she denied it.

"No, I'm not pregnant!" She would lie.

Eventually, after Bishop denied the rumors over and over again, LaMonica decided to believe him. Mainly because she herself had been the subject of rumors around the small town of Saginaw, rumors that were completely untrue. She figured if they would lie on her, they could lie on him too.

Somehow, ironically now, Bishop saying his mother accused him of being on drugs put LaMonica's mind at ease. If Bishop was telling her about it, didn't that mean he didn't have anything else to hide?

By the time LaMonica was off the phone with Bishop, he had convinced her to move back in with him. She hurried and gathered most of her and baby Monica's things again, and Bishop came to pick them up. This time, however, they didn't have an estimated time of arrival for Mama, so she left a lot of things behind, including baby Monica's formula.

She had a couple of packs in the diaper bag, but most of the formula for the entire month were on Mama's side porch.

When they got home on Norman Street, LaMonica informed Bishop that she only had enough formula for a few days because they left in such a hurry.

"You should have grabbed that, LaMonica."

"I know, but I can just go around there and get it tomorrow," LaMonica said.

"You know your mama's probably gonna be mad."

"Yeah, I know."

LaMonica knew it would be heavy lugging all those heavy cans around the corner the next day, but she had had to leave fast before Mama caught her and Bishop and turned into Batwoman again.

18

THE FORMULA

Early in the morning, LaMonica left Monica at home with Bishop and walked around the corner carrying a large garbage bag to pick up the rest of the stuff from Mama's house that she had left, including Monica's formula.

When she got there, Mama was upset and wouldn't let her in.

"So, you done moved back around that corner with that nigga, huh?"

"Mama, I just came to get the rest of my stuff and baby Monica's formula."

"Where is the baby?"

"She's at home with her daddy."

LaMonica carried on this conversation with Mama while she stood on the stairs. Mama only spoke to her through a crack of space she held in the screen door. When she went to grab the handle to come inside, Mama closed the door in her face and locked it.

"You ain't coming up in here. Everything you need is around that corner."

"But Mama, I need the rest of my stuff."

"Everything you left here stays in this household."

"What about the baby's formula? I need my baby's formula."

"Like I said, everything in this house stays in this house."

LaMonica left the front of the house and walked to the side porch where she knew the baby's formula was. Mama hurried up and locked the side door too, so she couldn't get in.

When LaMonica went to walk back home, she saw that Bishop was parked on Kirk Street between 5th and 6th Streets. He had come to give her a ride home so she wouldn't have to carry all those heavy metal cans. He had watched everything that happened.

"She won't give you the baby's formula?"

"Nope," LaMonica replied.

"Man, that's cold. That's out cold," Bishop said.

"LaMonica, I wouldn't even do that to my worst enemy. Keep somebody's baby's formula? Man, even if I didn't like the person, I would throw them the formula. 'Bleep here, take it.' Anythang. I mean, it's a baby; of course, she's gonna need her formula.

'I ain't neva' said this before LaMonica, but I'm saying it now: look yo' mama already dun called the people on you for nothin', If you deal with her after this, then you a fool. And I'm gonna be mad at you because she's doing this to OUR BABY!"

LaMonica and Bishop drove up to the WIC office to ask for more formula.

"I'm sorry, but we just gave you coupons for the whole month. We can't give you any more formula coupons until next month."

They then drove to the welfare building to ask for help.

Their case had been transferred to a new worker. The case-worker informed them that they couldn't get any help for formula; that's what WIC was for.

"I just left there. They can't help either."

"Well, then I suggest you use your check to buy formula this month."

"But then how am I going to buy diapers? And we've already spent most of the first half of the month's check, and the second doesn't come out until 2 weeks from now. I just have enough to buy the baby more diapers."

"Well, you should have your 3rd of the month Social Security check today. You can use that for formula," The caseworker explained.

"Her mama won't let her have that check," Bishop added.

"We have that dependent Social Security income right here in your monthly budget. We deduct that amount every month from your ADC benefits."

"Well, ma'am, can you please just add that back in because I don't have access to that money? My Mama won't give it to me."

"Doesn't the check come in the mailbox every month?"

"Yes. But it comes in my mother's mail to her address. I've been down to the Social Security office and asked them to change the address before, but they said only my mother can do it."

"Well, technically, you still have your mother's address listed on your license, so nothing is stopping you from retrieving it from the mailbox."

"I took it once from the mailbox. Now when she's home, she grabs it early, so I can't. And she has it set up that when she's gone, the neighbor from next door comes and takes it until she comes home."

"What's this neighbor's name?"

"Otis Wilson," LaMonica explained.

The caseworker looked up Otis Wilson in the phone book and saw that his address was next to Mama's. She called him and identified herself as being a worker of the State of Michigan.

"I have LaMonica Powers in my office telling me you hold her check on the 3rd of the month. Is that true?"

"Yes. Mrs. Powers asked me to hold both her and LaMonica's check when she's not home because she doesn't want her daughter having it."

"Well, I want you to know it's a Federal crime to mess with a mailbox. If I were you, I would stop that practice right now!"

And with that, the caseworker promptly hung up.

"Hopefully, next month, you'll be able to get it."

LaMonica and Bishop left thinking of a plan of how they were going to get some formula for their baby and more diapers.

"You know LaMonica, I wouldn't put it past yo' mama to call the CPS and say we don't have any formula."

LaMonica had enough formula for baby Monica for a few days, but she liked to keep a stockpile on hand. She thought about Jaqueline.

"Take me around to Jaqueline's house, and I'll see if she has any extra cans I can borrow."

Jaqueline gave LaMonica one can, but that's all she could spare. She promised to pay her back later in the month.

"That's why I don't get all my formula at once, just in case of something like this." Jaqueline lived in the house with a lot of people and didn't want to come up with cans missing.

"I know Jaqueline, but I was at my mama's house. I didn't think I had to worry about it."

Baby Monica was fine for now, but LaMonica preferred not to end up in a situation where she was scrambling for formula. The next day she and Bishop went to Abortion Alternatives, and they gave them three more cans of formula. Each can would last a day. So now baby Monica had almost a week's worth of formula.

As much as Mrs. Powers liked shooting guns at the range, she knew that sometimes the phone can be an even better weapon when you really need to get something done. She got on the horn and used every avenue available to her, starting with the CPS. She knew that the CPS would do a full search of LaMonica and Bishop's house if she called them out, including inspecting her food and formula.

"Child Protection Services, yes, this is Mrs. Ella Mae Powers. I've called you guys before regarding my daughter, LaMonica Powers and my granddaughter, Monica Holmes. I just don't believe it's safe over there at that house for the baby. If LaMonica refuses to come home, then at least the baby should be here with me where it's safe. I have everything she needs right here at my house."

"We will go out to check the home to see if it's safe, Mrs. Powers, but unless the child is in danger, we won't be removing her."

"I understand. Just please call me back afterward with the report. Thank you. Have a nice day."

The CPS showed up at LaMonica's door just like Bishop predicted they would. LaMonica and Bishop both welcomed them in and went through the same demeaning procedures as the last time. However, on this visit, the CPS worker wasn't so quick to close the case. Since Mrs. Powers called so frequently, her supervisor was now weighing whether they should escalate the inspection to the next level or not.

Within that same week, a friend of the family stopped by, Tonya. She came by the house at a time when Bishop wasn't home.

Tonya was a City Building Inspector. At first, LaMonica thought this was a personal visit. She didn't realize Tonya was there on official business.

"Your mom asked me to stop by. Can I look around and just make sure the house is safe?"

LaMonica didn't know how to say no to Tonya, so she let her look around. Tonya walked around writing on a notepad, making lists of things that were required to be repaired. She was moving so fast around the house, she left LaMonica in a daze. Somehow, she didn't piece together what was going on until Tonya was done.

By the end of it all, Tonya had a list of repairs that needed to be made in order for the house to be up to code and considered "livable," until then, the house would end up with a condemned sign and could not be occupied or rented out.

When Bishop returned, he was beside himself. LaMonica thought back. When she was angry at Bishop and went back to stay with Mama, she had let it out about some of the problems with the house. They weren't serious ones, but probably technical issues of the city. Mama had called this woman to have the house condemned. It was probably a personal favor to Mrs. Powers. She had sat there dazed all that time, just letting her go through the home and mark up that paper, citing issue after issue that would take money to repair.

"LaMonica, why did you let that woman in the house? Don't you know any better?"

"I don't know Bishop; I've known her all my life. I didn't think this was what she was doing."

"I'm going to have to let my family know about this. And now we may have to move."

Bishop and Alonzo had a third family member's name on their deed, an uncle. He agreed to do the repairs, but he would not have them done within the timeframe to keep the house open. The repairs added up to thousands of dollars. LaMonica and Bishop had no way to add any money to that. They were stretched enough just trying to get formula and diapers for baby Monica.

The frustration level came to a head later that week. Monica was down to one can of formula, and LaMonica only had enough money to either buy diapers or formula.

"There's no way I'm supposed to have to take the diaper money and buy formula when WIC gave me formula for the entire month for my baby. I need to buy her diapers with this money Bishop."

"So, what you wanna do?"

"I'm goin' around that corner and getting my baby's formula no matter what! That's what I'm gonna do."

"Okay, I'll drive you. And you should get your check too."

Bishop and LaMonica pulled up in front of the big yellow house on 5th Street. Bishop stayed out in the car parked on the street with the baby. LaMonica was angry, and she was knocking on Mama's door like it. Mama came to the door immediately.

"What's going on?"

"Give me my baby's formula. I need my baby's formula now!"

"Go on away from my door LaMonica."

"I'm not leaving here until I have my baby's formula, and that's a fact!"

"Oh, is that right?"

"Yeah, that's right! And you can give me my check while you're at it."

"Look, you and that nigga Bishop don't scare me. You'd better get on away from my house if you know what's good for you."

"Look, Mama, if you don't want to give me the check, that's fine. But I'm not leaving here without my baby's formula. You're gonna give me that toooooday!"

"I ain't got to give you nothin'. Now get on away from my house, LaMonica, before I call the police."

Bishop had the window down and was listening and watching all of this from the car.

LaMonica was infuriated. *How dare this woman keep my child's food from her? I'm getting it today, no matter what.*

She walked around to the side porch where she knew her baby's formula was and began kicking in the screen door to take it. She made it inside to the tiny side porch, and Mama came out there fast with her security guard nightstick. Before LaMonica knew it, Mama had her on the ground with her foot on her chest and was beating her everywhere with her security guard stick. All she had wanted was her baby's formula.

LaMonica couldn't stop what Mama was doing, she couldn't fight back, and she couldn't get off the floor. She just screamed and wailed in pain while Mama beat her all over with the nightstick. Bishop heard it from the car. He got out.

"Hey, hey. Stop it! Mrs. Powers. Stop it! Now I'm going to call the police." And he did. Bishop went around the corner to the store payphone and called 911.

LaMonica was stuck on the side porch getting beat on with a security guard stick almost as thick as a bat. It felt like forever. When Mama finally let her go, Bishop had made it back. LaMonica jumped in the car with him, crying and in pain.

"LaMonica, you'd better not EVER deal wit' yo' mama after this."

The car didn't move.

"What are we doing, Bishop? Let's go." LaMonica was rocking and rubbing her arms and legs, which were all on fire from being beaten.

"We're not goin' anywhere. We're waiting for the police to come. Yo' mama ain't getting away wit' that."

"Yeah, Bishop, you're right. She can't get away with this. I want her to go to jail. I can't believe she did this to me when all I wanted was my baby's formula."

Two cars from the Saginaw Police Department pulled up. One set of officers knew Mama personally. They asked her what happened separately from LaMonica. Then they questioned LaMonica, and she explained the whole incident to them. Bishop was a witness. He told them everything that had occurred. They had the rejection letters from WIC and the welfare office in the car to show that she wouldn't give LaMonica her baby formula.

A neighbor from next door told the police the truth when questioned, which sealed Mama's fate. She was going to jail. There was way too much evidence. Mama called everyone she knew on the police force all the way up to the Chief. The officers spoke to their superiors and all kinds of people at the department. They did not want to lock Mama up. They hemmed and hawed around. Bishop and LaMonica stayed on the premises, and they did not back down.

"Are you sure you wish to press charges on your mother?" the officer asked.

"Yes. I want her to go to jail for what she did to me."

"Just to be clear, you're choosing to press charges on your own mother?"

"Yes, sir. She needs to go to jail for what she did to me."

After LaMonica wouldn't change her mind and had witnesses to boot, law enforcement had no other choice but to take Mama to jail. That's an image LaMonica will never forget, them carting off Mrs. Powers to lockup. Mama hated criminals and fancied herself a police officer. This was hurting her pride more than anything.

The officers allowed Mrs. Powers to lock the house up first before they took her to jail.

"Officers, can I get my baby's formula now?"

"Everything's locked up, but if you have a key to the residence, I don't see why not. Besides, you're still listed as a resident here at this address."

"Okay, officer, I'm gonna take her home to get her key," Bishop lied.

LaMonica didn't have a key to Mama's house. She had relinquished it back when she moved out at 17 and had never gotten it again from Mama when she moved back in after her break up with Bishop.

"Don't worry, baby, I know how to get into that house. We'll get the baby's formula and anything else you want that's in there soon."

Bishop and LaMonica left and waited for the officers to clear out. They took baby Monica to Jaqueline's house so they could retrieve what they needed from Mrs. Powers' house. Instead of parking on 5th Street, Bishop parked on 4th, and they climbed the back fence. Bishop then used tools from Mama's garage to jimmy the back door. They were inside in a snap.

LaMonica directed Bishop to where Monica's formula

was on the side porch. He grabbed it and carried it out to the car on 4th Street. LaMonica then grabbed the remaining things she had left of her and Monica's from the house and placed them in a garbage bag to carry out to the car.

They both knew they had to hurry because they didn't anticipate Mama being held in lockup for long. She would be held for 24 hours at best, but possibly out sooner. The officer had made a report and said that if LaMonica was serious about pressing full charges, she would have to come down to the station and retrieve a copy of the police report. This would prompt the chain of command to send the case over to the Prosecuting Attorney's Office. LaMonica most likely was not going to go that far with the case.

When Bishop returned, he went to Mama's back room and said, "Let's take this TV she doesn't need in the back."

It was Mama's small old school black-and-white TV.

"Bishop, why would we need to take a TV? That's not mine."

"Look what yo' mama did. We could at least take this TV and get some money for it."

LaMonica didn't know what to think of Bishop for that. She didn't say yes or no, but she didn't agree with it. Bishop grabbed the small TV and took it with him as they left out Mama's back door.

The manner in which Bishop had removed Mama's back door made it unable to replace, so he just sat it up against where it originally went, and they left.

19

SURVIVING

B ishop pawned Mama's TV for a small amount of change.

"Are you going to get my mama's TV out of the pawnshop later, Bishop?"

"Sure, baby." He never did.

Mama never used the TV, but still, it didn't sit right with LaMonica how Bishop had just decided at the last minute to grab her TV. They were only supposed to be getting the formula and her personal things. Now she felt guilty, like she owed Mama an apology, even though she had just beat her with a nightstick.

LaMonica purchased diapers for Monica with the money she had left over from the check at the beginning of the month. Now that she had the baby's formula back, she called the CPS worker to let her know.

"Well, I'll have to come back out and do an inspection check."

The CPS worker came back out and did an inspection.

"My mother is just making these phone calls for spite.

Why do you guys keep coming out? Can't you stop doing this now that you see what she's doing?"

"Even if your mother or any anonymous person called us every single day and if we checked every single day and found nothing wrong, we would still have to come out."

"I mean, isn't this harassment at some point?"

"This is just the way the law is written in Michigan," the CPS worker explained.

Anna was working on a case and required to be in the courtroom. While there, she was given a list of files that were in line to be escalated CPS cases. Among those file names were her son's name and LaMonica's. The primary reason for this was because of Mrs. Powers' phone calls and Bishop's previous criminal history. Anna spoke with her colleagues and associates that worked inside the CPS and assured them that these were frivolous calls from Mrs. Powers and she had frequent contact with her grandchild and her parents. They immediately closed the case.

The next court case Anna attended was a criminal case. In that case, a witness implicated her son Alonzo while testifying, and the court stated they would be issuing a warrant for him.

One of Anna's colleagues who frequently worked as a liaison to Drug Court pulled her aside and showed her the long list of arrests both her sons had. Bishop's were mostly for petty crimes.

"Anna hun, just a heads up, but typically when these types of crimes are committed so frequently, it's usually to support a drug habit."

"Thanks for the information," Anna responded with humiliation.

Between her two sons being brought up in court at her job and the escalated case, CPS almost started on her granddaughter; Anna was thoroughly embarrassed and couldn't wait to speak to the both of them.

She invited her son's and their families over for dinner that day. Anna laid into everybody, including LaMonica. She said they all had embarrassed her at work that day, and now that she had cleared this up with the CPS in Monica's situation, she would be returning to her job in Detroit.

Anna knew that this is what Mama would try to pull in the first place, so LaMonica didn't get why Anna was upset with *her*. Now, Bishop and Alonzo, that was another matter. That one made sense. "Anna, I can't help it that my mama keeps doin' this."

"Well, every time you make up with her, you tell her too much of your own private business. You need to stop doing that, LaMonica."

Anna then pulled Bishop aside into another room and asked him point-blank, period, if he was on drugs (LaMonica had no knowledge of this). He denied it and was offended.

"Look, Bishop, you are showing a lot of signs, and you are pretty thin too."

"What? I've told you before, of course I'm thin. I'm thin like my daddy. I don't do drugs. How you gonna listen to them folks at work over me? I'm leavin'."

Bishop emerged from the back room after speaking to Anna. "Come on, baby, let's go!"

After clearing up the situation with the formula, LaMonica scrambled for a home to move into now that Mama had had Bishop's house condemned. Rent for apartments and homes on the East Side of Saginaw in the '90s ran about $350 a month plus deposit. That didn't include utilities.

LaMonica's monthly governmental welfare check was

$385 minus the $75 they deducted monthly because of the Social Security check that she didn't have access to. This obviously would leave her short.

It was the summertime, and LaMonica remembered a training program Mama had told her about called The Summer Youth Training Program. This program was an extension of the Job Training Partnership Act (JTPA). This government program was put into place by the Reagan Administration in the '80s and gave teens and young adults the opportunity to work at nonprofit organizations and receive a check. The weekly check didn't come from the nonprofits themselves but rather from the government training program. The only requirement to obtain these jobs was that the applicant be low income. Teens could choose between working as leaders for youth at Summer programs, working in the kitchen at nonprofits, or working in an office. LaMonica applied to work in the office at First Ward Community Center and was hired.

The remarkable thing about the JTPA program was that none of the income counted against mothers receiving assistance. LaMonica could receive money through working at a JTPA site and continue receiving welfare assistance. She was definitely starting to see that a plan to be on welfare was really no plan at all. Instead, it should be used as a temporary situation, not a goal to reach for - the way Bishop introduced it to her.

Bishop and LaMonica were in between a rock and a hard place again. Monica was getting low on diapers, and they needed the money that was coming in to move into a new home before the condemn date ended. LaMonica's job through the Summer Youth Training Program wouldn't start up for another two weeks.

Bishop asked his mother for money for diapers, but at

this point, she was skeptical of giving him any money (not being sure if he was using it for drugs or not). Of course, LaMonica couldn't ask Mama for help after everything that had happened.

Bishop had a plan.

"Baby, you don't got to worry about it. I'm gonna get our baby some diapers."

"How B?"

"I'm gonna break into some cars and get some radios, then sell them at the pawnshop for money. Come on, roll wit' me."

LaMonica felt pressed to the wall to get her baby some diapers, so she road with Bishop. She was about to see a glimpse of what Bishop does when he's not home sometimes at night.

They road way out to the suburbs to some luxury apartments. Bishop sat in the car in a dark part of the parking lot.

"You see that light right there? I timed it. It flashes on and off every 3-5 minutes. The next time it flashes off, I'm runnin' and grabbing radios."

"Alright," LaMonica responded.

The light flashed off, and Bishop took off. He was opening doors lightning fast. Some were unlocked, and some were locked. He got each door open with either a hanger or some sort of tool he had with him (LaMonica wasn't sure). She wondered how he was able to open those doors so fast now, but not back when he locked his own keys out of his car at the movies last year.

Bishop returned to the car before the security light could flash back on. He had on an old raggedy Winter coat, and the radios were stacked up inside of it from his pelvis all the way up to his chin.

How in the world did he do that so fast? LaMonica thought.

He seems well practiced at it. This must be what he does ALL THE TIME, she realized.

"Alright, baby, I got 'em," Bishop said.

The next day LaMonica went with Bishop to the pawnshop. He sold most of the radios, and they went and got diapers for Monica. This was not one of LaMonica's finer moments, but Bishop seemed to have no qualms with it. He even installed one of the radios in his own car.

LaMonica and Bishop went looking for a house or apartment to rent. They found one on Jefferson Street on the East Side of Saginaw for $350 a month. LaMonica explained to Bishop that the entire ADC/welfare check would be going towards rent, and they would still be short. She would have to pay $50 out of her part-time job money through JTPA.

Bishop finally agreed to get a job. "Okay, baby, I'll look."

As luck would have it, LaMonica ran into a childhood friend named Jessica at the grocery store. Jessica was also working through a JTPA program. She didn't have any children and was looking for an apartment to move into but couldn't afford rent by herself. LaMonica spoke with Bishop, and they agreed to move her in as a roommate. The home was only a two bedroom, but baby Monica wasn't quite one yet, and she still slept in the room with them in her crib anyway. So it worked out.

Jessica and LaMonica went half on the rent and deposit for the first month, and everyone moved in. Finally, the stress of where she and her baby were going to live was behind LaMonica, and she was enjoying her Summer job at First Ward.

Bishop had a friend who worked in Frankenmuth, Michigan, willing to help him get a job. Frankenmuth is a famous German tourist city in Michigan. Many Saginaw area residents who had low skill sets worked as dishwashers, cooks, and cleaners at the various hotels and restaurants in Frankenmuth. Bishop was hired as a dishwasher to work nights, and he could babysit Monica during the day when LaMonica worked. This would be somewhat new for him because he usually ran the streets all day. Mama had always watched Monica when LaMonica needed help.

Work at First Ward Community Center was awesome. LaMonica was finally able to be around other people her age. Bishop's car had broken down, so getting from on Jefferson Street (which was on the South Side) to the North Side was beginning to get hard. She had to scrap up on enough money to catch buses, taxis, and rides. Bishop knew a lot of people, and he would often secure rides for her to go to work, but that could get expensive.

On the plus side, he was really bonding with Monica watching her every day. It came to be that she favored her daddy over her mom a great deal. Previously, Mama usually watched her because she said they couldn't trust Bishop not to run the streets.

Once when LaMonica worked a temp job, answering phones, while they still lived on Norman Street near Mama, Bishop had babysat Monica while Mama had given her a ride to work. Mama had fussed at LaMonica all the way to that job about how she didn't think it was a good idea for Bishop to watch his own child.

"You should let that baby stay with me, LaMonica. Bishop don't know nothin' about watchin' no baby."

"That's her daddy, Mama. She'll be fine."

When Mama had dropped LaMonica off at work, she gave it some time and then doubled back over to Norman Street to check on the baby. Although she wasn't allowed within 300 feet of Bishop's house and definitely not on the inside—she still wanted to watch things from where she could.

Mama always had some sort of intuition about things. She rode through the neighborhood and found Bishop walking home from the store. She hollered at him from out of the window.

"Where's the baby?"

"I left her with my neighbor," Bishop lied.

Mama followed him and watched; no neighbor ever emerged from his house. She didn't buy his excuse. The moment she picked LaMonica up, she told her, "Bishop left the baby at home by herself, talkin' about he left her with the neighbor. Wasn't no neighbor inside his house. That nigga wasn't doin' nothin' but lying LaMonica. I told you not to leave that baby with him."

As soon as LaMonica made it home, Bishop knew she was upset.

"Look, baby, I ran to the store. The baby was in here in her crib sleep, and I didn't want to wake her up, so I asked the next-door neighbor, Diane, to keep an eye on the house while I was gone."

"She was fine, LaMonica. I was only gone for a minute to grab me a square."

"No, Bishop. She was not fine. How can Diane know what's going on with Monica from next door? Bishop, don't ever leave my baby alone like that again. Not even for a minute!"

"Okay, baby, stop trippin'."

"I'm serious, Bishop. If you need a cigarette that bad, carry her with you to the store."

Baby Monica started walking early at just 10 months. Now that they were at the new house on Jefferson Street, she moved around a lot. Bishop seemed to understand this, and

LaMonica felt confident that he wouldn't leave her alone again like that.

Bishop often had friends stop by, even in the new neighborhood. He tended to not have them in the house for long though. He seemed very protective of LaMonica and Monica. One of his friends stopped by one day when he was gone. LaMonica gave him the information that his friend had come by while he was away, and Bishop became very serious.

"LaMonica don't ever open the door when one of these niggas comes lookin' for me if I'm not home. A nigga could smack you and come on inside, rape you, and do anythang! Don't do that."

LaMonica thought, *what kind of roughnecks is Bishop running around with?*

A lot of the clues about what Bishop engaged in outside of the house, LaMonica would often put off to the side. She loved Bishop. He was her child's father after all. But she was watching him and his character and kept everything she saw in the back of her mind.

Bishop definitely wasn't used to working a typical job. The dishwasher job was the first legitimate job LaMonica had ever heard of him working. She was happy to see him leave for it and come home each and every evening. Until on about day three, he came home and said, "I quit!"

"You quit? Why Bishop?"

"Okay, baby, check this out. I'm washin' dishes, right? They dun showed me the ropes about where everythang is and everythang like that, right?"

"Right," LaMonica agreed.

"Okay, well, peep this. One of the machines was superhot, and they didn't warn me about that one being superhot. Now I put dishes on it and burnt myself."

"Well, did you talk to a supervisor about it?" LaMonica asked.

"Man, I talked to the one that trained me. 'Why would you tell me about everythang else I need to do here but not tell me that machine was hot?'"

"Baby, I'm done. I quit."

LaMonica just looked at Bishop. She was starting to lose more and more respect for him again. If she could work, why couldn't he? Her Summer job was ending soon. The rent on the house outweighed her welfare assistance check. Once the job ended, how was she going to buy things for Monica? How were they going to live with no money?

20

BACK TO SCHOOL

W hen Alonzo would come over to the new house on Jefferson Street, he wouldn't really come inside. He knew how LaMonica felt about him in general. Usually, he would just pull up, and Bishop would either sit with him in the car, or they would ride off somewhere.

One evening Bishop sat in the car with Alonzo. They were both really excited about a new opportunity. They were so enthusiastic that Alonzo came into the house with Bishop.

"Yo' check this out, baby. Lonzo has somethin' interesting to tell you about."

Alonzo has something interesting for me? LaMonica thought. she was all ears for this one.

"Yeah, check this out, LaMonica; it's a new computer school in Flint takin' students. They're giving bus rides every mornin' from Saginaw to Flint. But we can all ride together, just chip in on gas. Anytime we can't do that, we can always catch the bus."

"Man, you can get a good job with a Computer Programming Degree. My cousin went there, and now he just got hired to work at a bank," Bishop added.

"Okay, I like computers. What do I need to do?"

"The school officials are gonna be over at the Downtown hotel this Thursday. We can all go down there and fill out an application. You can also apply to get a loan. You can get thousands of dollars. Be ready Thursday mornin' around 8:00a.m., and I'll come pick ya'll up."

LaMonica was really looking forward to this. But if she and B were both going to go to school, who was gonna watch the baby? LaMonica was very particular about who watched baby Monica. She had rarely asked anyone other than Mama to babysit, not even her roommate Jessica.

Quite honestly, despite everything that had happened, Mama was the only person LaMonica trusted with Monica for long hours. Of course, Aunt Frieda could take good care of Monica, but she was older and had difficulty walking and getting around. Asking her to watch Monica for longer than 2 hours would be too much on her. B's mother would be at work during the day – not that she really watched Monica anyway. Nope, if she got into computer school, the only person to ask would have to be Mama. *Well, let's wait and see if I get in first*, LaMonica thought.

It was LaMonica's last week working through the Summer Youth Program at First Ward. She let everyone know she wouldn't be in that morning because she would be taking a test for school. Some of the workers had let her know that the Job Training Partnership Act program started up again in the Fall for students who were attending school. LaMonica kept that in mind.

That Thursday morning, Alonzo came and picked Bishop and LaMonica up. Aunt Frieda agreed to watch baby Monica for a couple of hours while they all applied for school. The school was packed with students from Saginaw filling out their school applications and Financial Aid forms. Once LaMonica filled out her application, she was called to a desk to speak with a counselor.

"I see here that you're 17, and you don't have your high school diploma or GED yet?" the counselor noted.

"Yes, sir, that's correct. Can I still go to college?"

"Well, you can if you are considered independent."

The counselor gave LaMonica a questioner that asked questions about whether she lived on her own or had a child. According to everything that she checked off, she qualified as independent.

"Okay, you've passed that round. Now we just have to have you take a test to see if you can benefit from school even though you don't have a high school diploma or GED. This is a technical hoop you have to pass for Financial Aid."

LaMonica began taking the test. At first, she thought it would be some kind of serious college entrance exam or something. Immediately she saw that it was just a formality. The questions on there were so easy that you would have had to have flunked out of elementary to get them wrong. One question even asked who the current President was. Very oversimplified stuff. The goal of the counselors was to get the students into the program.

The school was called Programming Systems Institute or PSI. The institute had two different pathways, Data Entry and Programming. The trade school entrance counselors said that all of the first semester classes were the same for both pathways. Students could choose how deep they wanted to go after that if they were undecided. Data Entry was training for more administrative positions, and Programming was preparing for higher level jobs in computers.

LaMonica's excitement level was at 100,000. She was going to train in computers for a real job that would pay the bills. Just then, the counselor came over to her. He said in order for her to proceed and qualify for Financial Aid (at 17 years old), she would have to get a signature from her parent. This meant she would definitely have to go and see Mama.

The counselor handed her a form for Mama to sign and gave her the date for the following week that he would be back in Saginaw to pick it up. Just as LaMonica was leaving, she spotted Luchie's cousin Mark. "Hey Lah Moan ee kah," Mark hollered.

"Who is that?" Bishop quickly asked.

"Oh, that's just Luchie's cousin, Mark. Bishop, it's cool."

LaMonica had to reassure Bishop because he could get quite jealous at times. Like that time, they spotted the group – *Ready for the World* at the mall, and LaMonica got excited like all the other teen girls.

"Oh, so you want to get excited about a singing group while I'm standin' here? B%# run on then!" had been his reaction.

Bishop seemed to be taking this pretty cool, though, because he would have never suspected LaMonica to be attracted to a Mexican boy. Little did he know she carried on a whole first love affair with Luchie's other cousin Juan back in the day. But in Bishop's eyes, because this guy wasn't Black, he didn't have anything to worry about. Which, in truth, he didn't. LaMonica only thought of him as Luchie's cousin and nothing else.

"So, are you gonna go to school in Flint?" Mark asked.

"Yeah, me and my boyfriend are all signed up."

"You know Genevieve goes there too?" Mark said. Genevieve was Luchie and Amalia's older sister.

"No, I didn't know. I haven't been in my mom's neighborhood or talked with Luchie and them in a while. How's everyone doing?"

"Oh, there doin' good. Yeah, I can see why you haven't been over there in a while. I heard about what happened with your ma."

"Yeah," LaMonica responded.

"LaMonica, it's time to go," Bishop said in a serious tone.

LaMonica knew she had pushed it with having so much conversation with Mark.

"Bishop, I've got to go by my mama's and have her sign these papers."

"Yeah, I heard the counselor," Bishop replied.

"Lonzo, let's bend this corner and head on around to 5th Street right quick."

Alonzo, Bishop, and LaMonica pulled in front of the big yellow house on 5th Street. Just as LaMonica got out of the car, Bishop asked her, "You sure you gonna be okay in there, baby?"

"Yeah, I'll be fine. It's been a while. Things have calmed down now."

"Well, if you're gonna be fine, me and Lonzo are gonna bend this corner and go check on the work being done on the house on Norman Street while you talk with yo' mama. I'll be right back, though."

"Okay." And with that, LaMonica went and knocked on the door. Bishop had Alonzo pull off when he saw Mrs. Powers at the screen door.

"Hi, Mama."

"Hi. Come on in."

LaMonica followed Mama down the hallway into the living room. She stood in the doorway.

"Have a seat," Mama suggested.

LaMonica sat in the chair near the window, where company usually sat. She didn't sit all comfy on the couch like she would have before the incident.

"How's the baby?"

"She's doing good. She's walking now."

"Walking? Wow! Boy, they grow fast."

"Yeah, they do."

"It's been a while since I've seen her."

"She's with her Aunt Frieda right now. Me and Bishop just signed up for college in Flint."

"Oh really?"

"Yes. It's a computer school. I saw Luchie's cousin, Mark, and he told me Genevieve goes there. I can get a degree in Data Entry or Programming. I just have to get a parent's signature since I'm not 18 yet." LaMonica handed Mama the form.

"You need me to sign this?" Mama asked.

"Yes, Mama, that's the only way I can go to school."

"Let me get my glasses."

Mama read over the form and signed it.

"Here you go."

"Thank you."

"So, who's gonna watch the baby if you and Bishop are both going to school?"

"I'm not sure yet," LaMonica said.

"Well, you might as well bring her over here. I'm home every day."

It wasn't like Mama to apologize, and so she didn't. Her way was to usually do favors. That was her apology.

"Well, Mama, I'm sorry for breaking your door?"

"And Bishop made off with my TV."

"Yeah."

"Well, don't worry about it. It's in the past."

"Where ya'll livin' at now?"

"We moved over on Jefferson Street."

"What's the address?"

LaMonica gave Mama the address to the house.

"Okay, well, maybe I'll stop by and see you and the baby some time."

"Okay, Mama."

LaMonica saw that Bishop and Alonzo were outside, and she went and jumped in the car.

"How'd it go, baby?"

"It went good. She signed my paper, and she's gonna watch the baby while we go to school."

"Okay, okay," Bishop said.

They went and picked Monica up from Aunt Frieda. When they got there, LaMonica and Bishop played a few rounds of cards with her and then headed home.

21

COMPUTER LOVE

S chool started in August, and LaMonica, Bishop, and Alonzo headed to PSI in Flint. The first day of school was very exciting. There were four classes that LaMonica and Bishop attended. Computer Skills, Typing, Business Communications, and Microsoft Disk Operating System (MS-DOS).

MS-DOS was the most interesting and also the most complicated. Back then, computers didn't come with point-and-click tools or GUI graphics. You had to use command codes to program every action you wanted the computer to take. If you wanted the computer to save a file (to a floppy disk), you typed in a command code (there was no save button to push).

Typing and English Business Communications were also fun for LaMonica. This whole thing seemed to be right up her alley. She loved getting out of the house to learn a new skill, plus she always loved computers as a kid.

For each class, she sat right next to Bishop and spoke to him and him only. Typically, LaMonica would be talkative, especially in a school environment. Somehow her personality had changed since being with Bishop. She no longer was her true self anymore. LaMonica was now quiet and followed Bishop's lead on everything, almost to the point of having no real public opinions of her own.

Immediately in MS-DOS class, a group of girls approached Bishop and Alonzo. They were beautiful Mexican girls who appeared to be happy and free. Bishop and Alonzo were very popular in certain groups in Saginaw. Very often, women would speak to him while he and LaMonica were out. Sometimes he would introduce her and say, "this is my woman, LaMonica." Sometimes he would not. Most often, he wouldn't, but they got it. It was very ironic how it was fine for Bishop to be free to speak with anyone but not so much for LaMonica. Although, she never heard any rumors of him doing anything wrong with any women.

Going to PSI every day had become LaMonica's only outlet. She was hungry for knowledge and geeked up about the things she was learning. Luchie's sister Genevieve attended the afternoon classes. Bishop and LaMonica attended the morning classes, so she only saw Genevieve in passing.

Genevieve had started attending PSI long before LaMonica did. It was almost time for her to graduate. One morning when LaMonica was leaving morning classes and Genevieve was entering, she informed her that she was near graduation and had a job ready as a Bank Manager thanks to her training at PSI. She also had done some internship work through PSI and directed LaMonica to check in with the counseling office.

This thrilled LaMonica and gave her so much hope. People were actually getting decent jobs after training at PSI. She was determined to stick with it. Genevieve had chosen the Programming route, but LaMonica remembered her days of Programming class back in Oklahoma. It wasn't something she was too thrilled about. Besides programming, every command on the computer had gotten cumbersome.

Now Data Entry, that was something LaMonica could really get behind. The faster her typing speed became, the more excited she got. LaMonica didn't have a computer or a typewriter at home, so the Typing class teacher had given her a QWERTY keyboard printout to take home and practice with. She had practiced typing the home row keys, jkl; and asdf repeatedly with it. Then she began to type her name (using only the paper printout at home).

She practiced on that QWERTY paper every day after school until she could type L-a-M-o-n-i-c-a without looking. After just two weeks in typing class, LaMonica had already learned that the letters outside of asdf and jkl; were the letters you had to reach for and build dexterity.

LaMonica's name was pretty long as names go, she discovered while typing. Learning how to touch type it helped her memorize so many reaching letters and build dexterity at a much faster pace. By the end of week two, she was already at a 35 words per minute (w.p.m.) typing speed. That was the minimum for most office jobs.

LaMonica was now ready to ask the office for an internship on Monday. But if Alonzo and Bishop would have their way Monday at PSI would never come. On the drive home from class that Friday, Alonzo had some news.

"Yo B, we don't need to keep coming down here. I found out from a girl I know in there; they don't even give you your loan check to cash. They use the whole thang on paying for classes here. She said when her $3,000 check came in, they held it right there in the office and made her sign it over to them."

"Man, that's some bull," Bishop said.

"I know right," Alonzo agreed.

"Nawl man, we're done with this school," Bishop said.

So that had been their only reason for attending? LaMonica thought. *They thought they were going to get some money. And now that the money was off the table, they were done with it.* Well, LaMonica wasn't done with it. She still wanted to go to PSI. She would let Bishop know when they were home alone too.

LaMonica could hardly maintain herself. As soon as they had picked up Monica and made it home, LaMonica had begun.

"Bishop, I still want to go to PSI."

"Why? They take your whole loan check and make you sign it over to them."

"Is that why you wanted to go to school, Bishop? For the loan check?"

"Nah, I'm just sayin' it ain't right though."

"I want to get my Data Entry Certificate, Bishop, and I'm going to see if I can start doing an internship at First Ward."

"Ain't no money in no internship, baby. And besides, Lonzo said he ain't going back, so you don't have a ride all the way to Flint no way."

LaMonica didn't want to quit computer school. She was enjoying it, and she was becoming quite good at it. She thought back to when Alonzo said the school had a bus that transported students from Saginaw to Flint. Also, during orientation, the school counselors had brought that up. They informed all of the students from Saginaw that they had a bus that would pick them up from the Downtown Mall in Saginaw and drive them to and from school. They emphasized that they didn't want students dropping out because of transportation issues.

"Bishop, I can get down there on the bus."

"Okay, baby. I guess." Bishop tried very hard to discourage LaMonica from continuing on with computer school. He felt that since he had dropped out, there was no need for her to go. But since she was this serious about it, he would let it go. He had always told her he would give her enough rope to hang her own self.

LaMonica spoke to Mama. She was willing to come and pick her and baby Monica up every morning, transport LaMonica to the Downtown Mall, and then pick her up again in the afternoon and give her a ride home. She would babysit Monica too. Now there was no excuse for Bishop to hold her back.

Bishop said he was going back to hustlin' in the streets during the day. LaMonica just listened to his plans without agreeing or strongly disagreeing with him. She did let him know she didn't agree with making money that way. Something deep in her heart told her God would not bless a person financially doing "hustles." She told Bishop as much.

"Bishop, you see, every time you try this kind of stuff, it never works out. Maybe because this isn't what God wants you doing?"

Bishop talked a lot about the bible and believing in God. Since the time he and LaMonica had gotten together, he had spoken about how his mother and father had become very religious church members and turned their lives over to God. He said he believed in God strongly but didn't believe in half steppin'. "I ain't half steppin'. If I'm gonna give my life to God, I'm gonna do it all the way." Until then he would just live how he wanted to live.

Bishop seemed to believe that he would just do everything else until then. LaMonica felt like she could do the right things that God was placing on her heart now and not wait for perfection to come. She often warned Bishop that his schemes could not be blessed. He wasn't really trying to hear it, though. So, this time when Bishop said he would be hustlin' during the day when she was at school, she decided not to fight him on it too much.

Monday morning LaMonica rode the Programming Systems Institute bus down to Flint. She sat on the bus by herself. When she made it to school, she sat by herself also. Since Bishop wasn't there, she knew no one, and she spoke to no one.

Most of the students in attendance were much older than her except for the three pretty Mexican girls who knew Bishop and Alonzo. They were always laughing and joking with each other. They were like those pretty popular girls you always saw and heard coming down the hall on high school TV shows.

During the lunch break, LaMonica headed down to the counselor's office and told them she was ready for an internship.

"Okay, we can try to place you for an internship, but to be honest, we have more connections with organizations in Flint than we do in Saginaw," the counselor explained.

"If you can find an organization willing to accept you, we can give you credit for it, and it'll even shave off $1,000 from your tuition."

"Yes, but couldn't I get a work-study position?" LaMonica asked.

"Well, you didn't fill out for work-study on your Financial Aid application. That's something you can try for next semester. But if you find an organization, give them this form so you can get credit."

LaMonica already had it in her mind that she would see if she could work in the First Ward Community Center office for her internship. She had already worked there during the Summer for the Summer Youth Training Program, and she and Mama knew everyone in charge, so getting in should be a breeze.

After school that day, Mama took LaMonica up to First Ward. The Director immediately signed the slip she needed for PSI. Everything was going great. She would begin working in the office as a receptionist, answering phones and typing as needed.

For the next few days, LaMonica continued to ride quietly alone on the bus and sit quietly alone in class. Sometimes a couple of the Mexican girls from class would ride the bus and sit together and sometimes, they would carpool together and drive down to Flint. It seemed they carpooled together more often than they rode the bus.

By the fourth day of LaMonica sitting quietly alone in class, one of the Mexican girls who knew Bishop and Alonzo approached her.

"Hey, where's Lonzo and B? They don't go here anymore?"

"No, they stopped coming."

"Well, you don't have to sit here by yourself. Come sit with us."

Come sit with us can be a profound statement—an offer of inclusion. The pretty Mexican girl introduced herself as Marciana. Marciana then introduced LaMonica to her two friends Torie and Bella. They all had bubbly personalities like Marciana, but it was clear that Marciana was the leader.

There are times when you meet someone that will introduce you to your destiny in life. Little did LaMonica know that by meeting Marciana, she was on the road towards her true destiny.

Marciana was so different from LaMonica. She was free. No one told her when to be home or where she could and couldn't go. She was free to go and do anything. Before meeting Marciana, Torie, and Bella, LaMonica never left the school building for lunch, even though PSI was on Saginaw Street near Downtown and the Flint Pavilion with a hub of restaurants and activities going on. For one thing, she knew Bishop wouldn't like it, and for another, she didn't want to miss the bus going back to Saginaw.

"Come have lunch with us, LaMonica," Marciana urged.

LaMonica usually just grabbed a honey bun and a soda pop from out of the school vending machine.

"Where are you guys having lunch?"

"We're probably going to hit up one of these restaurants around here."

LaMonica thought to herself; hopefully, she could find something on the menu that was inexpensive because she didn't have much money for lunch.

They went down to Halo Burger, which was well known in Flint for its supreme burgers and extra-large milkshakes. Luckily LaMonica found something on the menu she could afford and sat down and ate with the other girls. These were some of the happiest girls LaMonica had ever seen. All of them still lived with their parents, and none of them had any children. They were just free. Free to go to school, work, out to eat, anywhere they wanted to.

LaMonica hadn't sat down like this and just had fun like a young person in a long time. Aside from back in the Summer when she was working at First Ward through the Summer Youth program, LaMonica hadn't had much time to spend with people her own age.

Most of the students from Summer at First Ward had returned to high school or went off to college. The other interns were either older than her or held the same responsibilities if they were her age. Day in and day out, they took care of a home and took care of a child. None of them were free, like Marciana, Torie, and Bella.

LaMonica's friends rarely came by her house on Jefferson Street because they were all in their last year of high school and had to obey their parents. Many of their parents didn't approve of Bishop, especially after the things that Mama had told them. Jaqueline would sometimes come over and visit, but that was rare because she lived on the North Side closer to Mama. Some of LaMonica's friend's parents had out and out told her that when she goes back home to live with Mama, they would feel more comfortable letting their daughters visit.

LaMonica didn't have to work as an intern at First Ward on Fridays, so she sat there eating her Halo Burger and Fries, enjoying a lost moment of a teenager being out with her girlfriends. She knew the bus heading back to Saginaw had long since left. Marciana had already offered for her to ride back with them in Torie's car.

LaMonica called Mama on the payphone to let her know she didn't need to pick her up at the Downtown Mall. She would be getting a ride straight to her house from a friend. Mama was fine with it.

"Okay, Mama, see you soon."

"Is everything okay? Do you need to hurry home to pick up the baby?" Marciana asked.

"No, everything's fine." LaMonica knew Mama was fine with her staying out to eat with her friends, but Bishop, that would be another story.

By the time LaMonica made it home to Bishop with

Monica, it was much, much later than she would typically arrive at home. As soon as LaMonica pulled up, Bishop was ready and waiting.

"Where you been, baby?"

"I missed the bus, so I stayed after school. Marciana and some of her friends gave me a ride."

"Who is Marciana?"

"One of the Mexican girls that you and Lonzo were talking to in class."

"Oh yeah, they were friends with Jeffrey's girl."

"I wish you would've called and let me know you would be this late. I was worried about you."

"Well, I used all my change to call Mama."

"Oh, so you just gonna call yo' mama but not me, huh?"

"Bishop, I had to call my mama because she had Monica."

"Yeah, okay, whatever, LaMonica."

LaMonica, Marciana, Torie, and Bella continued to hang out together at school, often riding home with each other. Sometimes, they would catch the bus. As the school year progressed, Bella dropped out of class, and then it was just Marciana and Torie. Then eventually, Torie dropped out, and it was just Marciana and LaMonica left attending classes.

PSI had a high dropout rate. Their certificate program was an exorbitant cost. Most of their students were from Saginaw, and most of them were economically disadvantaged and qualified for Financial Aid. This would later prove problematic for PSI.

LaMonica began hanging out with Marciana after work during the week and after school on Fridays. Marciana's mother eventually bought her a small used car. She and LaMonica began riding back and forth to school together every day. LaMonica hadn't had so much fun since before she became a parent. Sometimes Marciana would come over to Mama's house, and they would watch movies together. LaMonica wouldn't return home to Bishop until late in the evening.

She began staying at Mama's house longer and longer after work and school. She would call and check in with Bishop, but she would wait until the last possible moment to come home. Things had begun to be unpleasant there. LaMonica's roommate Jessica's job had ended after her first month of paying rent. She said she was looking for work, but there didn't appear to be anything on the horizon. Bishop never worked again, and his "hustles" still didn't bring in any money. And to top it off, her Aunt Felisha (Daddy's sister) was pushy and had moved in upstairs.

22

AUNT FELISHA

L aMonica still hadn't spoken with her father. She hadn't spoken with him the whole time she was pregnant, and now Monica was turning one soon. It had been nearly two years since he put her out of his house and said she wasn't his daughter anymore because she wouldn't have an abortion.

Oh, she had run into him since that time, and she had even been to his house (while he was at work). LaMonica's brothers Chuck and Malcolm had moved out of town with their mother, Birdie. During the Summer, when school was out, they came to visit Daddy. Since Birdie lived out of town, LaMonica had nowhere to visit them except at Daddy's. So, when he would be at work on 3rd shift, LaMonica would visit with Chuck and Malcolm while Daddy's girlfriend Linda and LaMonica's new baby sister NeKeisha would be there.

Nothing had changed between her and Daddy, though. LaMonica had even taken to referring to him as "Mr. Price" when anyone asked her about him.

"Oh, I don't know how Mr. Price is; I haven't seen him in a while."

Linda had two houses. One she maintained with Daddy and one she rented for her daughter Tondra and her child.

Back when it was NeKeisha's second birthday, Linda hosted it at her second home and invited LaMonica to come and bring Monica. Daddy was just pulling up as LaMonica was getting out of the car carrying baby Monica in her car seat. As soon as he saw LaMonica, he screeched out of the driveway in disgust without even attending his own daughter's birthday party.

Back when Mama had first started letting LaMonica visit with Daddy, he had warned her of her Aunt Felisha.

"Don't ever let yo' Aunt Felisha get too close. She'll rob you. She and her boyfriend just recently stole my TV."

LaMonica gathered that Aunt Felisha was on drugs after all the stories she had heard about her. When she and Bishop first moved into the house on Jefferson Street, she happened to be walking by and saw that the upstairs apartment was for rent.

"Ooooh, Ima see if I can rent the upstairs, that way, I can be right upstairs from my niece, and you can babysit yo' little cousins sometimes."

Aunt Felisha had two little girls that she often left with other people for days. She had once told Birdie she was running to the store for 30 minutes and couldn't be found until three days later to take care of her children. As cute as they were, that was the last thing LaMonica needed.

Bishop met Aunt Felisha. They seemed to click. They say people recognize their own type of people and game recognizes game.

"Oh yeah. You should move in that apartment upstairs; that way, we'll know who our neighbor is," Bishop said.

Bishop ran into the house to retrieve the phone number. LaMonica didn't know what to do if she ran into the house to warn Bishop it would look weird to leave her aunt standing outside, but she didn't think inviting her inside the house was the right idea either.

Bishop came back all smiles and handed Aunt Felisha the landlord's phone number. "Here you go."

"Thank you, baby. Can y'all give me a reference?"

"Oh yeah. Oh yeah! We gonna hook you up. Don't worry about it. As soon as the landlord asks us about you, we'll give you a good reference," Bishop said.

LaMonica knew, based on Daddy's warning, that this was a horrible idea. When Aunt Felisha left, LaMonica immediately told him not to give the landlord a good recommendation.

"Bishop, my daddy told me never to trust Aunt Felisha. Don't give her a good reference to the landlord."

"Okay, baby, I won't."

This is all Bishop said on the subject. He didn't ask any further questions about Aunt Felisha or why she wasn't trustworthy. He just agreed with her right away, so LaMonica thought everything was fine. Imagine her surprise when two weeks later, Aunt Felisha was moving in.

"Bishop, I thought you were gonna tell the landlord not to let Aunt Felisha move in?"

"Baby, I did. I guess she didn't listen to me," Bishop lied.

When Aunt Felisha moved in upstairs, she brought all kinds of hell with her. The home wasn't an apartment in the traditional sense. It was a whole house, and the upstairs had been converted into an apartment. There was a flimsy door with a weak lock on it downstairs. Aunt Felisha was always opening it up and asking to borrow this and that. Food, laundry detergent, all kinds of things. Her daughters had a pair of skates that they would take turns sliding across the floor on in the evenings during dinner time.

Aunt Felisha was pretty open with what she did for extra-curricular activities and for money. She didn't try to hide it at all. She smoked crack rocks, and she sold "tail" to make money to get it.

Even though Aunt Felisha was so open about using drugs and prostituting, she frequently lied to get the money for those habits.

The hell and the lies started up right away. One night when Bishop was gone, Aunt Felisha was using the front porch of the house as some sort of makeshift whore house pick up and drop off point. This was unbeknownst to LaMonica, however.

"LaMonica, it's a nice warm night; why don't you come and sit outside with me."

LaMonica came outside. She decided that maybe she should give her aunt a chance. After all, lending and borrowing household items was considered neighborly. Up until that point, Aunt Felisha hadn't done anything extreme (other than the irritating sounds of her daughters skating). LaMonica decided she would stop being so biased against her because of what Daddy said and give her a chance.

While LaMonica and Aunt Felisha were sitting on the porch commenting on the beautiful stars and night sky, a car pulled up.

"I wonder who that is?" LaMonica said.

"Oh, baby, that's just my trick. I need to run off and make me a lil' money, so I can get me a lil' somethin' to make me feel good. I'm gonna leave the girls here while I take a ride wit' him. They're upstairs sleep. You'll be here to watch over them while I'm gone, won't you?"

"Aunt Felisha, I can't do that. I have to stay down here with Monica in case she wakes up."

"Oh, baby, you don't need to go upstairs. They're not gonna wake up. I'm just lettin' you know just in case. They should be sleeping all night. Besides, I won't be gone that long. This one ain't got that much money."

Aunt Felisha said this as she was easing off the porch and jumping into the dark Cadillac parked in the driveway. LaMonica was not okay with this, and Aunt Felisha hadn't even waited for her response.

"Aunt Felisha, wait!" LaMonica hollered.

"I'll be right back, baby." Aunt Felisha hollered out the window.

Surprisingly Aunt Felisha did return in less than 30 minutes. LaMonica hadn't been sure she would after all the times she had heard of her leaving her children for days. Maybe they were just rumors, but Birdie wouldn't lie, would she?

As Aunt Felisha was pulling back in with one trick, two tricks were pulling up in the driveway for her. All of these cars were nice Cadillacs and Buicks. No doubt, GM Plant men.

Aunt Felisha had to explain to one trick that she would be back soon so he wouldn't leave.

"Oh hey, I'm gonna run with him for a minute, but I'll be right back. Stay here on the porch and talk to my niece."

What the hell does she mean stay here and talk to my niece? LaMonica thought. She hoped this guy didn't get the wrong idea. He was clearly half drunk.

"I just wanna let you know that I'm not into all that stuff that my Auntie is into."

"Oh, nawl, I wouldn't think you would be."

"Oh, alright."

He just stood on the side of the porch against the railing, making small talk until she pulled back up with the last gentlemen.

"Okay, come on, baby, I'm ready."

"I'm getting ready to go in the house Aunt Felisha," LaMonica said annoyed.

"Okay, baby. This my last one. I'll be going upstairs in a minute."

~

*T*he warmer it got, the more LaMonica started running into friends and family on the South Side. Just sitting on the porch could turn into a real social affair. The house on Jefferson Street was in a prime spot on the South Side of Saginaw. On the weekends, when LaMonica was off from work or school, she was sure to run into someone if she sat on the porch. A lot of the friends and family that were young like her she hadn't seen in a long time. Most young guys didn't come over to the North Side near 5th and Kirk, where she and Mama lived because of enemies and other gangs.

One particular Saturday, while sitting on the porch, her cousin Corbin was walking by. Corbin was related to LaMonica from Mama's side of the family. He had a good heart, but he was always in and out of either jail or prison, usually for fighting and shooting with rival gang members or most likely selling drugs. Often times Mama would listen on the police scanner and hear the police chasing after him.

"They after that Corbin again, LaMonica," she would say.

Corbin was from the South Side, so he never really came over to the North Side of town. Whenever he wasn't locked up, LaMonica would see him at family gatherings. she loved him and had grown up very close with him and his sister when they were children before gang sides of town were so important.

On this bright and warm Saturday, Corbin stopped when he saw LaMonica sitting outside on the porch with Monica.

"Hey cuz, this you?" (meaning, is this where you live?)

"Yeah, this is me."

Bishop came outside and shook hands with him.

"Come on in."

For some reason or another, Aunt Felisha kept prying the lock off the door that connected the upstairs from the downstairs and coming back and forth into LaMonica's apartment. She could peep down the stairs and see what was going on whenever she wanted too.

When she heard Corbin's voice and saw him, she wanted his attention right away. Corbin was young and dressed in the latest styles from the hood. He looked like he had money and possibly drugs. Aunt Felisha sniffed this out ASAP.

"Aye, Aye, come here real quick. Let me talk to you." She was calling for Corbin.

LaMonica already knew what she wanted. "Don't go, cuz. She doesn't want anything."

He started walking towards the stairs anyways. LaMonica was so embarrassed. She had heard of the instances of women offering oral sex and everything else for drugs. She just knew that's what Aunt Felisha was up there trying to do. *Oh, my goodness, this is so embarrassing.*

Corbin came back down the stairs. LaMonica didn't know whether they had had a transaction or not. She didn't really want to know.

Later in the week, Aunt Felisha came and asked LaMonica to babysit.

"LaMonica, can you watch the girls while I go get my furniture from my old house? My ex-boyfriend just agreed to let me come get it. It won't take long. You know your little cousins are about tired of sleepin' on pallets and stuff. They need their beds."

LaMonica agreed to watch the girls for a few hours so Aunt Felisha could go to her old house and bring back her furniture. She decided she would trust her since the last time she left, she had come back on time.

"Don't you need a truck to get your furniture?" LaMonica asked.

"Oh, nawl, me and my ex are on good terms now. When I get over there, he'll let me load up his truck, and I'll be back. It won't take long, baby."

The two girls came downstairs with LaMonica. She played board games with them, fed them lunch, and they played with Monica and her toys.

"It won't take long" turned into dinner time. LaMonica had expected it to take a couple of hours to move furniture, but now six had gone by. The girls were behaving fine, but LaMonica was concerned. Nighttime rolled around, and LaMonica found something for the girls to watch on TV. The girls fell asleep on the sofa. Saturday turned into Sunday. LaMonica began getting concerned. What if Aunt Felisha hadn't made it back by Monday when she had work and school?

LaMonica called up Birdie long distance. "Birdie Aunt Felisha has been gone since yesterday, and I still have both of the girls."

"That's why I can't watch Chrisette and Basia anymore. They are really nice girls, but their Mama doesn't come and pick them back up. The last time I watched them, Felisha said she was running around the corner "real quick," and she didn't come back for a week."

"A week!" LaMonica exclaimed. "I thought it was just a couple of days."

"No, it was a whole week," Birdie said.

"I can't have them here a whole week. I have to go to work and to school tomorrow!"

"Well, I'd suggest you call your Aunt Bren and see if she can come and pick 'em up. And learn from this, don't say yes next time."

LaMonica called Aunt Bren.

"Aunt Bren, Aunt Felisha has left Chrisette and Basia here since yesterday afternoon."

"When did she say she would be coming back?"

"She was supposed to pick them up after she went and got her furniture yesterday. She said she would only be gone a couple of hours, and she never came back. I have to go to work and school tomorrow, and I'm not quite sure what to do. I'm thinking about calling the CPS."

"No, don't call the people on her. If she hasn't made it back by this evening I'll come and get them. Are they alright?"

"Yes, they're fine. They've eaten and have been playing with Monica, but I just don't like the way she did this."

"I know, chile, it's a shame. She dun did this sort of thang before. She'll be back after a while," Aunt Bren said.

"I'm glad you called LaMonica. I've been wantin' to get in touch with you anyways. Felisha called me the other day saying you needed help. She claimed you didn't have no money to buy the baby no diapers but had too much pride to reach out."

"What? No, Aunt Bren, that is not true. Monica is over here fine."

"I thought it wasn't nothin' but Felisha trying to scam somebody out of some money. I asked her for your phone number, but she wouldn't give it to me, talkin' bout, 'No, don't call LaMonica. She doesn't want nobody to know. I don't want her to know I asked for help for her.'

'She dun called yo' daddy, yo' grandma, and everybody else huntin' up on some money, tryna use you as an excuse to get it."

"Well, she should have known better than to try to use me as an excuse with my daddy. That wasn't gonna help her at all."

"You and Chuck still ain't talkin'?"

"No, Aunt Bren, I haven't spoken to 'Mr. Price'."

"Mr. Price." Oooh wee, chile no, you didn't call yo' daddy that. Don't worry, though. He'll come around as soon as he sees that pretty baby."

Aunt Bren had been the first one in Daddy's family to come to see LaMonica and baby Monica at Mama's house when she made it home from the hospital.

Aunt Felisha finally made it to the house to pick up her kids Sunday night. Apparently, she had spoken to her sister because she knew LaMonica had been on the verge of calling the CPS.

"I don't need nobody callin' the CPS on me. Chrisette and Basia are all I have in this world. That cocaine is hard to get off of. I've been on it since I was a young girl. But I love my babies. Nawl, niece, that ain't how family does. You don't have your own family taken away. You must have got that stuff from Mrs. Powers because we don't do that."

Aunt Felisha carried Chrisette and Basia, who were asleep up the stairs one by one.

23

IT'S NOT GOOD IN THE HOOD

L aMonica continued her daily routine of working at First Ward as an intern and going to school in Flint at PSI. Her roommate Jessica still had not found a job, and Bishop was "hustling" and not bringing any money home per usual.

Marciana lived on the South Side, so Mama would come and pick Monica up every day. Then LaMonica and Marciana would ride together to Flint. After school, Marciana would give LaMonica a ride home, or sometimes they would catch the bus depending on if Marciana's car was running or not. It was a really old car and often had issues.

After all of Mama's fussing for LaMonica to have an abortion, Mama had turned out to be Monica's biggest fan. Often, she would ask LaMonica for her to spend the night, and when Bishop and LaMonica wanted her home, they would have a hard time getting Mama to bring her back. She spoiled baby Monica something awful, too, often letting her get her way on everything. When LaMonica was trying to wean Monica off the bottle, Mama would sneak and give it to her. When Monica threw a tantrum and wanted to sit in her front-facing car seat in the front of the car, Mama would let her.

Mama would let Monica have her way at almost anything she wanted. LaMonica had tried to put her foot down on the things that were a safety concern. In particular, she asked her to "please stop placing Monica in the front seat of the car." Mama liked Monica up in the front seat so she could talk to her better, and it was her preferable way to spend time with her while driving. LaMonica had continued to insist that it was unsafe for her age.

One late afternoon Mama came to pick LaMonica up from work at First Ward. Baby Monica was seated in her front-facing car seat in the front, of course. LaMonica didn't feel like arguing with Mama or hearing Monica have a fit because she had become used to riding in the front. She usually chilled at Mama's house with Monica after work since she dreaded going home most days. Despite her frustration with Monica being in the front seat that afternoon, LaMonica reasoned that since Mama didn't live too far from First Ward, it would be fine. She would just arrange Monica the proper way when it was time for the ride back home all the way to the South Side.

Because First Ward was set dead center in the projects, the neighborhood could be problematic, just like Mama's neighborhood. As Mama and LaMonica made their way down Norman Street with Monica seated in the front passenger seat in her car seat, they ended up being in a line of cars at the stop sign between 6th and Norman in front of Bishop's old house.

Mama's car was the 4th car in the stop sign line up, to be exact, and there were cars behind her. The driver from the car directly at the stop sign exited his car and began shooting at the car that was directly behind him. The driver in the car that was behind the car getting shot at was the 3rd car in the lineup and directly in front of Mama's car. They began slamming on the gas in reverse to get away from the gunfire and, in turn, were slamming into Mama's car over and over again.

Mama was trapped because of the cars behind her. LaMonica was screaming because she didn't know what to do. *How could she get down low for safety, knowing her baby was sitting right in the front closest to the gunfire?* She tried undoing her car seat while staying low, but because of her nervousness, she couldn't get it unbuckled. LaMonica began screaming at Mama.

"Back up! Back the F*** up!"

Wham, the car in front would slam into them again.

"Look, LaMonica, I'm not gonna tear my car up backing into folks like this fool."

"YOU'RE ALREADY GETTING YOUR CAR TORE UP FROM THE FRONT ANYWAY! LOOK, MY BABY'S LIFE IS MORE IMPORTANT THAN YOUR CAR!

'I TOLD YOU TO STOP PUTTING MY BABY IN THAT FRONT SEAT! I TOLD YOU THAT A LONG TIME AGO!" she continued screaming.

Mama was trying to maneuver out of the situation, but every time she tried, she was hit again by the car in the front.

Finally, the gunman got back in his car and left. The whole thing probably lasted just minutes, but it felt like forever. The driver of the car who had been shot at emerged from his vehicle with his friends. He checked himself. He was unscathed. All of his friends were fine, and they began ignorantly laughing at the situation. LaMonica recognized the driver who had gotten his car shot up – a boy who used to live in Mama's neighborhood and fathered a child with one of her friends.

His car was shot up, but he and his friends were unscathed. LaMonica, Monica, and Mama were fine, but Mama's car was torn up. Her hood was bent up like a mountain. It had a crest in the middle, and she had to look out of the side of the window in order to see how to drive home. Mama's car was also smoking and knocking. It was all she could do to make it around the corner.

As soon as they pulled into the driveway, LaMonica grabbed Monica from the front seat and hugged her. She was fine, not really even upset by the commotion. LaMonica loved being at Mama's house, but she wished she would move out of that stupid neighborhood.

"See, Mama, I told you, you should move from over here!"

"LaMonica, you sound crazy. I'm not leavin' my house!"

Growing up, LaMonica had always thought of Birdie as a second mother, and so since she partially blamed Mama for the danger Monica had just been in, she desperately wanted to talk with her. As soon as she got inside of the house, she called Birdie and told her what happened.

"LaMonica, you need to try and get another job away from the projects. It's bad over there."

"Yeah, you're right," LaMonica told Birdie.

"You know your brothers are coming there soon to visit your dad."

"No, I didn't know that."

"Yeah, they'll be there for the whole Winter break."

Monica's first birthday was in the Winter.

"Oh, good, well then maybe they can come to Monica's birthday party with NeKeisha and Linda."

"Man, I wish I could be there for my grandbaby's first

birthday. She ain't even gonna know who I am." Birdie said this in the whiny baby voice she often used.

"That's okay though, I've got a surprise coming for you. I'll be seeing my granddaughter soon; just you wait."

"What kind of surprise?" LaMonica asked.

"I can't tell you. If I told you, it wouldn't be a surprise."

"Come on now, I can't stand not knowing."

"Okay fine, I'll tell you," Birdie said.

"Me and your brothers are moving back to Saginaw in a few months."

"Yay! I can't wait."

"Nobody knows but you, so keep it hush-hush for now."

"Okay, I will."

"Alright, do you want to talk to your brothers?"

"Yes."

"Alright, here they are. Te amo."

"Te amo," LaMonica replied back.

Birdie was half White and Half Mexican. She made a habit of saying I love you in either English or Spanish whenever she ended conversations with family and friends. She had taught Chuck and Malcolm to do the same.

LaMonica talked with Malcolm because he was the one she was the closest with. Chuck was usually the quiet one. Girls loved that about him, that he was the handsome, strong, silent type. Malcolm was the sanguine personality type, a social butterfly that brought everyone together. He was the singer like Daddy and the jokester. He was very popular. People around town often recognized LaMonica by saying, "Oh, aren't you Malcolm's sister?"

Malcolm hopped on the phone.

"So, are you coming with Linda and NeKeisha to Monica's birthday party?"

"Are there gonna be any chicks there?"

"Malcolm, it's a child's birthday party."

"Aye, some of their mamas might be there lookin' for a man."

"No, Malcolm. It's at my mama's house. There won't be a lot of people."

"I'm just playin' wit' you girl. You know I'm comin' to my niece's first birthday party. But I'm bringing my own playlist."

"Okay, Malcolm, hahaha." Malcolm was hysterical to talk to.

Chuck and Malcolm both told LaMonica, "I love you," and then they all hung up on the phone.

Mama was watching all of this. She didn't mind LaMonica having a relationship with her brothers, but she didn't particularly care for how close she and Birdie were. Besides, she was itching to call some of the repair shops before they closed.

Mama had been in the background the whole time saying, "LaMonica, when are you gonna get off that phone. I need to call AAA before they close."

Mama called AAA insurance and the police and told them it had been too dangerous for her to stay on the scene of the accident. The insurance company had the car towed to a shop. There were all kinds of fluids leaking out of it, and when you tried to start it up, it smoked badly.

There was no doubt about it; LaMonica and Mama would have a rough time getting around now.

24

ALARM CLOCK

urphy's Law says, "if anything *can* go wrong, it will," and Mama always said, "when it rains, it pours." That's just what happened. After having the car towed and looked at, Mama found out that not only would the car need a new hood, but it would need a new motor as well. She had it towed to at least three different mechanic shops, and they all told her the same thing. She even let Bishop's mentor, Carter the mechanic from the hood, look at it. He had the same prognosis. She needed a new motor, which would cost over a thousand dollars to buy and have installed. Mama's deductible for these types of accidents was also $1000, so the whole thing was a wash and a bust.

To top it off, Marciana's little putt-putt car had gone kaput, and she would be catching a ride to the Downtown Mall and riding the bus to school in Flint every day like LaMonica.

LaMonica decided she didn't know if working at First Ward in the projects was worth it. In fact, she was working as an intern, so she didn't even get paid. Then she remembered the JTPA program and that they paid for teens to work and go to school.

LaMonica took a day off from School and First Ward and rode the bus to the Community Action Center (CAC), where the Job Training Partnership Act (JTPA) counselors were located. When she arrived, they were very open to placing her at a paid job site. She had worked through them before at First Ward during the Summer Youth Training Program and did a good job.

Since she brought in her schedule from Programming Systems Institute and all income documentation, the counselor was very enthusiastic. She could choose to stay at First Ward Community Center in the office or choose to receive paid training at the County Court House in the Prosecuting Attorney's Office for Child Support.

LaMonica was thrilled about the prospect of working at the courthouse in a Prosecuting Attorney's office. She accepted the assignment from the JTPA counselor and was told all she had to do was interview well with the Office Manager directly in the Prosecuting Attorney's Office for Child Support.

She called her friend Kristina and told her the exciting news. Kristina had visited LaMonica a couple of times since she moved over on Jefferson Street, but her mother, Mrs. Belk, was one of the mom's that felt much more comfortable with her daughter being at Mrs. Powers' house for a visit than where LaMonica lived alone with Bishop.

Mrs. Belk was sophisticated in her style and dress. She wore Channel perfume and expensive clothes. She often put her and Kristina's hair up into a French roll when they had important events to attend. LaMonica knew that would be just the perfect thing for an interview at the courthouse.

Mrs. Belk came and picked LaMonica up from home

and brought her over to her house in Sheridan Park. LaMonica and Kristina spent time together, and Mrs. Belk showed LaMonica how to do her hair in a French roll.

Mama was still doing security jobs on the weekends. One of her security team co-workers, James, had an adult son in his 30s who had just moved back home with him. His name was Big Jimmy. Big Jimmy was dating LaMonica's friend Jaqueline.

Mama spoke with Big Jimmy, and he agreed to pick LaMonica up from school in Flint directly on her interview day so she wouldn't be late. Mama would, of course, pay him for driving back and forth to another city.

Mama and LaMonica had the babysitting all planned out. Mama would catch the bus from the North Side in the morning down to the bus center Downtown. LaMonica would catch the bus with Monica from the South Side to the Downtown bus center. Then LaMonica would hand baby Monica off to Mama to babysit and get on the transfer bus to the nearby Downtown Mall.

Everyone was doing their part as a team, everyone except Bishop. Bishop still "hustled" all day and came home in the evenings with no money. LaMonica was again finding it harder and harder to respect him. With all the work she was doing to be a productive member of society, Bishop couldn't/wouldn't even try.

At this point, she was holding on to him because they used to be deep in love, and he was all she had ever really known. He was her child's father. Bishop was the first man that she consciously had ever had sex with. In her mind, he was the one she gave her virginity to. That incident with Chester was sick and crazy the more LaMonica thought about it.

But other than a teenage love, what was holding her and

Bishop together still? They weren't fighting to be with one another for love anymore. LaMonica was 17 going on 18 now. Nobody could stop them. And so, quite frankly, the whole relationship had become boring from LaMonica's perspective.

They were both disappointed in each other. Bishop threw hurtful words at her nearly every day.

"You ain't a real woman. You ain't nothin' but a teeny bopper."

Bishop would say this because it was all the organization LaMonica could handle to work a job and go to school while catching buses between two cities without a car. She and Monica often ate at Mama's house with Mama. She got around to cooking once she made it home late in the evenings.

Sometimes her roommate Jessica would have already cooked in the house. Jessica had even taken to leaving the door open between the upstairs and downstairs, allowing Aunt Felisha to freely roam downstairs and even cook in LaMonica's kitchen. Every time LaMonica returned home, more and more of her meat and groceries would be missing from the freezer.

Bishop would try to stay gone until LaMonica was home. He claimed Jessica was looking at him like she wanted him and that whenever she cooked, her motive was to impress him. LaMonica found it hard to believe that anyone besides her wanted Bishop. None the less he would harp on.

"Look at this girl tryin' to look at me and cooking for me. You ain't doin' yo' job as a woman LaMonica. A real woman is supposed to take care of her man. You're supposed to be washin' my clothes and cookin' my dinner. But you can't cuz you ova' at ya mama's house eatin' and only worried about washin' you and Monica's clothes.

'Look at Renee and Becky how they take care of their man. Nawl scratch that Becky's White she can't cook so she don't count. Neva' mind about her. But baby, look at Renee, now that's a real woman. She takes care of her man.

'Or look at my cousin Carena, when her man got locked up, she was out here runnin' his dope business for him. Man, I bet you if I got locked up, you wouldn't even know how to run my hustle for me."

"No, Bishop, I sure wouldn't and wouldn't want to know how either." *Maybe Bishop really does sell drugs and not use them*, LaMonica thought – after he made that statement.

"Bishop, I'm working and going to school and taking care of Monica. I don't have time for all of that. I try to cook when I get in, and on the weekends, when I'm home."

"LaMonica workin' and going to school ain't no excuse. A real woman makes time for her man. Hell, look at my mama now that my daddy dun came back home. She works FULL TIME all the way in Detroit."

Bishop started getting more animated at this point.

"My mama cooks my daddy's breakfast befoe' she leaves for work, AND she cooks lunch. All he got to do is warm it up. Then she comes home and cooks dinner. Nah, that's a real woman. You ain't nothin' but a teeny bopper. You ain't no real woman. You don't even take care of yo' man."

LaMonica was getting to the point where she couldn't stand Bishop. "Bishop, you don't even have a job or help pay anything around here."

"That's cuz I'm out here hustlin' baby."

"But you never bring any money home, Bishop."

"These niggas be robbin' me half the time, baby. Then I got to pay to re-up (buy more drugs to sell). Baby, I told you it's gonna get greater later. One day I'm gonna drop money on you by the thousands."

Bishop moved in to hug and touch LaMonica.

"Bishop, don't touch me."

Bishop, even touching LaMonica, was starting to make her skin crawl. He would often blame it on her controversial birth control device, the Norplant.

"Baby it's that thang you got in your arm. That Norplant. It's messin' wit' yo' hormones. You're not even actin' like yourself no more."

Maybe it *was* the hormones in the Norplant. All LaMonica knew was that she couldn't stand to have Bishop trying to get intimate with her anymore. It was all she could stand to give him a kiss when he asked for one lately.

LaMonica was floored when recently his mother suggested they have a second child.

"LaMonica, Monica is getting bored. She won't get into as much stuff if you have another one to keep her company. That's the only reason we had B was to keep Lonzo company."

LaMonica had been working hard going back and forth between Flint and Saginaw, school and work, washing clothes at Mama's, and taking care of Monica and all of her financial needs to boot. Bishop had been zero help, and LaMonica told her as much.

"Anna, your son doesn't help me take care of this one. Why would I have another child with him?"

"Yeah, I understand that," Anna quickly replied. She couldn't argue with that one.

LaMonica swore in her mind. *For all the high levels of degrees Anna had and career success, what was she thinking? Maybe she just meant another baby; perhaps she didn't mean with Bishop.* LaMonica thought.

Both Anna and her husband Alonzo Sr. often said they were so proud of all the positive things LaMonica was doing.

Aunt Frieda also would remark the same thing. Some of Bishop's own family had pulled LaMonica to the side and told her she was too good for him. They couldn't even believe he had snagged her quite frankly.

That's because she was young and naïve when she met Bishop, but she was starting to wake up.

25

NEW BEGINNINGS

O n the day of LaMonica's interview, she got up extra early and fed, washed, changed, and clothed Monica. She had to dress her in tons of clothes because it was frightfully cold outside in the snow that day. LaMonica placed Monica in her triple fat sweatsuit outfit. Then she placed her in her snowsuit. It was like having two snowsuits on. There was no way Monica was going to get cold while they were out there catching that bus.

She did her hair in the French roll that Mrs. Belk taught her and wore her Easter suit with stockings. She put on leggings to wear while traveling and her boots. Then placed her heels in her purse. She would probably get cold because she wasn't wrapped up like an "Alaskan baby" like Monica but hoped the bus wouldn't take too long.

LaMonica held Monica and rocked her back and forth for warmth while clinging onto her purse and diaper bag. When the bus finally came, she had to maneuver everything around to get to the change she needed to pay to get on the bus.

While riding the bus, LaMonica thought about how Bishop had always tried to make her feel lucky that she even had a boyfriend who stood by her side after they had a baby. Like she had won some prize for having a man who didn't have other kids with other women. Her self-esteem was so low, she halfway believed him.

LaMonica had been with Bishop since she was 15 years old. She thought about that day that she ran away from home tired of whoopings, tired of Ms. Demona's verbal abuse, tired of Mama. Some would say she ran from the frying pan into the fire.

During the nearly three years that she had been with Bishop, he had almost eroded whatever self-worth she had. Often telling her if she left him, she wouldn't find anybody but someone who wanted to use her for a check. She halfway believed him on that too. She saw it all around her with his friends and family, especially with Alonzo and his poor wife, Becky.

Bishop WAS one of the few black men in the hood that she knew who had only one "baby mama." Although they never referred to each other like that. That was a promise they had made to each other. That they would always be together as boyfriend and girlfriend. They would never be "baby mama" and "baby daddy" to one another.

Now that LaMonica was about to be 18 soon, getting married didn't seem like a priority to either of them anymore. But as much as Bishop disappointed her as a partner, Monica loved him. When he was home in the evenings, he spent a lot of time with her. They laughed and played games. She became excited at the very sight of him from the moment he stepped through the door. She couldn't take that from her, plus Bishop was all LaMonica had truly ever known. Deep down, she loved him even if she was irritated by him.

On the flip side, the more LaMonica educated herself and elevated, the more she became disappointed in him. This debate with herself on Bishop would have to wait because LaMonica had made it to the Downtown bus center and Mama was there waiting for the baby hand off.

Like a football game, they were off for the touchdown. Mama had made it into the zone first because the North Side was near Downtown. As soon as LaMonica made it there with Monica, Mama was there to grab her and her diaper bag and catch the next bus home to 5th Street.

LaMonica caught the bus headed to the Saginaw County Court House. She sat in the back and took off her leggings, and put on her heels. The bus stop for the Court House was right in front of the building. The sidewalks were cleared of snow for the county residents. LaMonica stepped off the bus and into the building like she just arrived in a car.

"Dear God, please let me get this job," she prayed.

This wasn't like getting a JTPA assignment at First Ward, where everyone knew her and Mama. This was the Saginaw County Court House. Not everyone who interviewed would be picked. LaMonica had had some practice interview questions she worked on with the JTPA counselor. She hoped she could pull this off.

She entered the Prosecuting Attorney's Office for Child Support and interviewed with Susan, the Office Manager. Susan took to LaMonica right away. She liked that she was going to school for Data Entry and that her typing speed had reached 45 w.p.m. Susan gave her a typing test, and sure enough, LaMonica's typing speed was good. CAC didn't usually send girls over who had office skills already.

She felt she could train LaMonica on the county

computer system and told her if she wanted the job, it was hers. Then Susan introduced LaMonica to both of the attorneys in the office.

She had the job, *thank God*! Now she would be getting a check every week.

∽

inter break rolled around, and it was time for Monica's first birthday. LaMonica's brothers called her. They were in town and would be coming for Monica's party. Linda would be bringing her little sister NeKeisha too.

The Winter weather was horrible during the week of Monica's first birthday. LaMonica decided to have the party at Mama's house. Most of the people who were attending and didn't have cars lived near Mama. Plus, Mama had much more space at her house than at LaMonica's. And she could store food and preparations for Monica's birthday party there without worrying about it being stolen, like back at her house with Aunt Felisha running around.

Bishop was disappointed that the party would be at Mrs. Powers' house, where he wasn't welcomed.

"Why would you have her party at yo' mama's house when you know I can't go over there?"

"Bishop, it's just going to be easier over there. Jaqueline and her sisters can come from around the corner from Mama's house and bring their kids. And Mama found us a ride to gather up Monica's cake and presents from one of her friends at the Old Tymer's Club. They live on the North Side, and it'll all just be easier."

"Well, I guess my family can do something for her at my mama's house later."

"Okay Bishop," is all LaMonica would say. That would certainly be nice, but she knew good and well that Anna wasn't going to host a kids' party at her small ranch-style house, with its white leather sofas and glass everything, everywhere.

Anna did things for Monica on her own time and when she felt like it. Like for instance, she bought Monica a whole wardrobe of clothes during the Summer. Or she might get an urge and ask Bishop to bring the entire family by so she could visit with Monica. But a full-on kids' party was not something LaMonica could picture Anna doing. Bishop had always said that Anna liked to deal with kids when they were older, like his nephew, who she liked to take to Disney World on vacation. LaMonica guessed she would have to wait and see when Monica was older.

On the day of Monica's birthday, Mama, LaMonica, and Monica rode with Mama's friend from the Old Tymers Club. They went all the way out to Meijer's Shopping Center in the Saginaw Township to get Monica's cake. Mama took Monica to one end of the store while LaMonica found her presents and paid for them. She had them bagged up where Monica couldn't see. They grabbed the kind of food that kids liked and headed to the dollar store nearby.

LaMonica got Monica all kinds of games like pin the tail on the donkey and prizes for her party. She then picked her out balloons and streamers. All of this was making Monica very excited. Mama and LaMonica felt bad for Mama's friend, who had to drive home with all the balloons in her back seat.

Monica was jumping and playing with them while Mama would ask her, "How old is my pumpkin eater?"

"One," Monica would respond.

"That's right, you're one year old today Monica."

"You're a big girl Monica, give me a kiss," LaMonica said. Then Monica gave Mama and LaMonica kisses.

It was a perfect day.

When they made it back to the big yellow house on 5th Street, Mama and LaMonica decorated the stairs with balloons and streamers for the visitors to see when they came to the party. They put streamers up in the kitchen and got everything ready for visitors.

Jaqueline showed up first from around the corner on 3rd Street. She had her daughter, 10-month-old Alissa, with her, along with all of her nieces and nephews who lived with her. With Jaqueline and her crew alone, it was enough for a full-on party.

The kids were all having fun playing pin the tail on the donkey when Mama yelled, "LaMonica, your daddy's here."

"Oh no, Mama, that's probably Linda driving his car. She's bringing my sister NeKeisha and my brothers."

"I see your brothers LaMonica and a little girl. But I don't see Linda. LaMonica that's your daddy at the door."

"What!" LaMonica exclaimed. Daddy had not spoken to her in almost two years that couldn't be him. LaMonica ran for the door. All she could see was Malcolm and Chuck. She opened the door, and they both gave her a hug. And who was standing behind them carrying her little sister, NeKeisha? Daddy!

"Hey there," Daddy said and gave LaMonica a kiss on the cheek.

LaMonica couldn't believe it. Daddy was there.

"Hey Daddy," LaMonica responded.

"I brought NeKeisha by to celebrate with her niece."

NeKeisha was only 2 years old, but she was Monica's aunt. This was easy to forget because of their ages.

"Oh yeah, that's right, she is Monica's aunt." They both laughed as Daddy came down the long hallway inside.

LaMonica fixed her little sister a plate, and after she ate, she jumped right in with the other kids playing and having fun.

True to his word Malcolm had brought his own playlist of music, which were not generally thought of as children's songs. They weren't bad songs, though. They didn't have any cuss words in them, just radio versions of the hottest R&B songs and dance songs from the '90s.

After the games, the kids were all high on sugar from the cake and ice-cream, running around throwing streamers and confetti. Monica ran past Daddy a few times.

"Boy my grandbaby is a pretty little thang. I mean she's a pretty little thang."

Daddy went out to the car and got himself a drink. LaMonica was glad. This meant he felt comfortable at her mother's house. *He might even sing some old-school Temptations or James Brown songs.*

NeKeisha, Monica, and all the other kids were in a line running, jumping, and dancing to the music with laughter. Monica passed Daddy again. Daddy was in awe of her. He swished his drink around and raised his voice up a little louder, and said-

"Boy, my grandbaby is a pretty little thang, ain't she? You know what, LaMonica, that would have been a terrible thang for you to get rid of her. I'm glad you didn't listen to me. I'm glad she's here."

Order Snakes in the Mix: Book Three Now on Preorder

Snakes In

THE MIX

The Mixed Girl Series
Book Three

LAMONIQUE MAC

SIGN UP FOR MY NEWSLETTER

Be the first to learn about LaMonique Mac's new releases and receive exclusive content for fiction readers.

www.authorlamoniquemac.com

THANK YOU

I hope you enjoyed reading this book as much as I enjoyed writing it. If you did, I'd sincerely appreciate a review on Amazon, Goodreads, and BookBub. Reviews are crucial for any author, and even just a line or two can make a huge difference.

ABOUT THE AUTHOR

LaMonique Mac is an Amazon Best Selling Author. She writes in the genres of Christian, Young Adult and Nonfiction. She's also a publisher and a writing coach based in "Roll Tide" country Alabama with her family.

The books she has written and published are known for having a southern flair.

She can be spotted coaching new authors on how to write, edit, and publish on YouTube at Author LaMonique Mac.

LaMonique
Mac

 instagram.com/authorlamoniquemac

 facebook.com/lamoniquemac

 twitter.com/LamoniqueMac